DOROTHY L. SAYERS

STRIDING FOLLY

WITH A NEW INTRODUCTION
BY ELIZABETH GEORGE

nel

NEW ENGLISH LIBRARY
Hodder & Stoughton

First published in Great Britain in 1972 by Victor Gollancz Ltd
First published in paperback by New English Library in 1973
Hodder and Stoughton: a division of Hodder Headline
A New English Library paperback

17

A CIP catalogue record for this title
is available from the British Library

ISBN 978-0-450-03340-7

Typeset in Sabon by Hewer Text Ltd, Edinburgh
Printed and bound by
Clays Ltd, St Ives plc

Hodder Headline's policy is to use papers that are natural, renewable and
recyclable products and made from wood grown in sustainable forests. The
logging and manufacturing processes are expected to
conform to the environmental regulations of the country of origin.

Hodder and Stoughton
A division of Hodder Headline
338 Euston Road
London NW1 3BH

The greatest detective novelist of the golden age was born in Oxford in 1893. She was one of the first women to be awarded a degree by Oxford University and she was a copywriter in an advertising agency from 1922 to 1929. Her aristocratic detective Lord Peter Wimsey became one of the world's most popular fictional heroes.

Dorothy L. Sayers also became famous for her religious plays, notably *The Man Born to Be King*, which was broadcast controversially during the war years, and her translation of Dante's *Divine Comedy*. She died in 1957.

New English Library is the paperback publisher of all her detective stories and of two new Lord Peter Wimsey novels by Jill Paton Walsh. *Thrones, Dominations* and *A Presumption of Death* are based closely on and include some of Dorothy L. Sayers' own work. Hodder and Stoughton's Sceptre imprint is the publisher of the revised and updated version of the definitive biography, *Dorothy L. Sayers: Her Life and Soul* by Barbara Reynolds.

BY DOROTHY L. SAYERS

IN NEW ENGLISH LIBRARY PAPERBACKS

CONTENTS

CONTENTS

NOTE

Two of the three final Lord Peter Wimsey stories, *Striding Folly* and *The Haunted Policeman* were previously published in *Detection Medley*, edited by John Rhode (Hutchinson & Co. Ltd.), in 1939. *Talboys*, written in 1942, has not been published before.

I came to the wonderful detective novels of Dorothy L. Sayers in a way that would probably make that distinguished novelist spin in her grave. Years ago, actor Ian Carmichael starred in the film productions of a good chunk of them, which I eventually saw on my public television station in Huntington Beach, California. I recall the host of the show reciting the impressive, salient details of Sayers' life and career – early female graduate of Oxford, translator of Dante, among other things – and I was much impressed. But I was even more impressed with her delightful sleuth Lord Peter Wimsey, and I soon sought out her novels.

Because I had never been – and still am not today – a great reader of detective fiction, I had not heard of this marvellous character. I quickly became swept up in everything about him: from his foppish use of language to his family relations. In very short order, I found myself thoroughly attached to Wimsey, to his calm and omnipresent manservant Bunter, to the Dowager Duchess of Denver (was ever there a more deliciously alliterative title?), to the stuffy Duke and the unbearable Duchess of Denver, to Viscount St. George, to Charles Parker, to Lady Mary. . . . In Dorothy L. Sayers' novels, I found the sort of main character I loved when I turned to fiction: someone with a 'real' life, someone who wasn't just a hero who conveniently had no relations to mess up the workings of the novelist's plot.

Dorothy L. Sayers, as I discovered, had much to teach me both as a reader and as a future novelist. While many detective novelists from the Golden Age of mystery kept their plots pared down to the requisite crime, suspects, clues, and red herrings, Sayers did not limit herself to so limited a canvas in her work. She saw the crime and its ensuing in- vestigation as merely the framework for a much larger story, the skeleton – if you will – upon which she could hang the muscles, organs, blood vessels and physical features of a much larger tale. She wrote what I like to call the tapestry novel, a book in which the setting is realised (from Oxford, to the dramatic coast of Devon, to the flat bleakness of the Fens), in which throughout both the plot and the subplots the characters serve functions surpassing that of mere actors on the stage of the criminal investigation, in which themes are explored, in which life and literary symbols are used, in which allusions to other literature abound. Sayers, in short, did what I call 'taking no prisoners' in her approach to the detective novel. She did not write down to her readers; rather, she assumed that her readers would rise to her expectations of them.

I found in her novels a richness that I had not previously seen in detective fiction. I became absorbed in the careful application of detail that characterized her plots: whether she was educating me about bell ringing in *The Nine Tailors*, about the unusual uses of arsenic in *Strong Poison*, about the beauties of architectural Oxford in *Gaudy Night*. She wrote about everything from cryptology to vinology, making unforgettable that madcap period between wars that marked the death of an overt class system and heralded the beginning of an insidious one.

What continues to be remarkable about Sayers' work, however, is her willingness to explore the human condition. The passions felt by characters created eighty years ago are as real today as they were then. The motives behind people's behavior are no more complex now than they were in 1923 when Lord Peter Wimsey took his first public bow. Times have changed, rendering Sayers' England in so many ways unrecognizable to today's reader. But one of the true pleasures inherent to picking up a Sayers novel now is to see how the times in which we live alter our perceptions of the world around us, while doing nothing at all to alter the core of our humanity.

When I first began my own career as a crime novelist, I told people that I would rest content if my name was ever mentioned positively in the same sentence as that of Dorothy L. Sayers. I'm pleased to say that that occurred with the publication of my first novel. If I ever come close to offering the reader the details and delights that Sayers offered in her Wimsey novels, I shall consider myself a success indeed.

The reissuing of a Sayers novel is an event, to be sure. As successive generations of readers welcome her into their lives, they embark upon an unforgettable journey with an even more unforgettable companion. In time of dire and immediate trouble, one might well call upon a Sherlock Holmes for a quick solution to one's trials. But for the balm that reassures one about surviving the vicissitudes of life, one could do no better than to anchor onto a Lord Peter Wimsey.

Elizabeth George
Huntington Beach, California
May 27, 2003

Lord Peter Wimsey and His Creator

BY JANET HITCHMAN

A man might say it is strange that the best detective books of this century should have been written by women. In these 'women's lib' days when there is supposed to be no difference between the sexes no woman dare say it. And, in fact, there is nothing strange about it at all. Given education, and inborn ability, the mind of a woman – and here I risk being tarred and feathered as a traitor to my sex – is more convoluted than a man's, less side-tracked and better able to accept the impossible. I should qualify this by saying that women were only able to use their minds fully when they became generally accepted, early in this century, as worthy of education and as writers doing 'their own thing'. Less than a hundred years before the birth of Dorothy L. Sayers the Brontës and Mary Ann Evans had to publish their works under male sounding names (Currer, Ellis and Acton Bell, and George Eliot), in order to gain acceptance as serious writers. It was all right for women to write homely religious tales, *belles-lettres* and pretty poetry, but to acknowledge the authorship of anything which smacked of real life, of deep passions or sex, was considered extremely bad form. Society was horrified when it discovered that the author of *Frankenstein* was a woman, Mary Wollstonecraft Shelley, wife of the poet. Society had to be considered since it was the only section of the community which could read and therefore buy books. After the universal Education Act of 1870 however, reading was within reach of all, and by 1900 most of the population was literate. And they were not asking for pious homilies, but for books which held their interest: adventure, romance, and for the kind of book pioneered by Wilkie Collins and Conan Doyle – detection. So one may say that the world was waiting for Dorothy L. Sayers, Agatha Christie and Ngaio Marsh.

Dorothy Leigh Sayers was born in 1893. Her father was a clergyman and a classical scholar. From him she inherited her love of literature, the classics, and her knowledge of high Anglican procedure. One of her father's parishes had been at Wisbech and it was there she came to love the fens, with their loneliness, beauty and latent terror, which made such a marvellous setting for *The Nine Tailors*. She was a Gilchrist scholar of Somerville College, Oxford, that nursery of learned ladies, from 1912 to 1915, where she gained Honours in Modern Languages. At that time, although women were able to study for the courses and pass them with honours, the University of Oxford refused to confer degrees on the so-called 'weaker sex', so she had to wait until 1920 before receiving her M.A. She was not rich, and going to Oxford even with scholarships had cost money, so it was imperative that she should earn her own living. Like so many educated women of her time, she found very little open to her. Science or medicine would have taken further years of study and, anyway, her gifts did not seem to lie in these directions. The law always fascinated her, but here again, the cost and lack of influence blocked any road to the King's Bench. The obvious career was school teaching which she tried for a year at Hull Grammar School but she found teaching not only soulless but extremely ill-paid. Like so many women of high intelligence she never found it easy to cope with the less mentally well-endowed, into which category all children fall. She has been called a snob, and it is evident that intellectually she was, although it is possible she was quite unaware of it. She returned to Oxford for a time and tried publishing but, as her employer said 'she was merry, talkative and argumentative, clearly not designed by nature for the routine work of a publisher's office'. This same publisher brought out her first two works, slim volumes of verse entitled *OP I* and *Catholic Tales*. There are glimpses of her at Oxford at this time. She always had strange fancies as to dress – as do the female characters in her books – and a fellow writer, Doreen Wallace, remembers drawing for her a large Tudor rose in red material for Miss Sayers to applique to her home-made black dress. Miss Wallace also recollects an embarrassing walk with her down the High, which Miss Sayers took in great loping strides rendering, meanwhile, Bach in loud and not particularly melodious voice to the astonishment of the townsmen.

Then, strangely as it may seem to us today, this learned, somewhat eccentric lady became a copywriter in the firm of Messrs S. H. Benson Ltd. She stayed with them from 1923–31, by which time her creation, Lord Peter Wimsey, had given her financial security.

She was an extremely complex character. She loathed all the publicity which a popular novelist is bound to attract, often giving offence by refusing to open fetes, sign autographs, etc. Yet by her eccentricities and outspokenness she could not fail to attract attention. There is a story told of her that when she was dining with her equally famous contemporary she said in a voice so loud it echoed round the crowded room 'God, I'm sick of Wimsey. Aren't you sick of Poirot, Agatha?' Miss Christie's reply has not been recorded but she, of course, has more than one detective on her list. Dorothy L. Sayers did invent another, Montague Egg, a commercial traveller, who appears in quite a number of short stories. The stories are good and the character drawn to life – she must have come across many such while at Benson's – but he never caught the imagination of the public as did Wimsey.

It is difficult, as Conan Doyle found, to discard a character once invented and adored by the public – he becomes an alter ego and dogs one's footsteps through life. Even marriage, much more fatal to a romantic character – and Wimsey was as romantic as any – than death failed to finish him off as the stories in this volume testify. He lives today, sixteen years after his creator's death as strongly as ever. Indeed he has lately taken on a new lease of life, on television and radio, but more than ever in the form in which he first began, between book covers. Apart from short stories he has not appeared in any new work since 1938, and that was in the novel version of a play, written in collaboration with Muriel St. Clare Byrne in 1936. It was Miss St. Clare Byrne who introduced Miss Sayers to the theatre; a milieu in which she had hitherto relentlessly refused to place Wimsey. But once there she fell 'like Lucifer, never to rise again', for most of her work after that was concerned with drama. She wrote the *Zeal of Thy House*, still popular, and added new dimensions to radio with her religious sequence of plays *The Man Born to be King*. When she died in 1957 she was at work on a new translation of Dante's *Divine Comedy*. So Wimsey had fulfilled himself. He had done that which every author dreams of – enabled his creator to cast him off and to please herself as to what and when she wrote. But what of Wimsey, the unquenchable – practically disowned by his maker but not by his public?

In a book of essays *Unpopular Opinions** – so called because some of them had been rejected by the people who commissioned them, one by the B.B.C. because 'our public do not want to be admonished by a woman' – Miss Sayers writes:

> The game of applying methods of the 'Higher Criticism' to the Sherlock Holmes canon was begun many years ago by Monsignor Ronald Knox, with the aim of showing that, by those

* Gollancz – 1946, p. 7.

8

*methods, one could disintegrate a modern classic,
as speciously as a certain school of critics have
endeavoured to disintegrate the Bible. Since then
the thing has become a hobby among a select set
of jesters here and in America. The rule of the
game is that it must be played as solemnly as a
county cricket match at Lords, the slightest touch
of extravagance or burlesque ruins the atmosphere.*

Later in the same book she herself plays the game,
proving with the help of Cambridge University lists
and guides, which college Holmes went to, and
what he read there. But although Miss Sayers
played the game with Sherlock Holmes, she made
every effort to prevent us doing the same with
Wimsey by seeing that every facet of him was
documented by *her*. Most of the books are prefaced
by a 'Who's Who' type paragraph.

*WIMSEY, Peter Death Bredon, D.S.O., born
1890. 2nd son of Mortimer Gerald Bredon Wimsey 15th Duke of Denver, and of Honoria Lucasta
daughter of Francis Delagardie of Bellingham
Manor, Hants.*
*Educated: Eton College and Balliol College, Ox-
ford (1st Class Honours, school of Modern History 1912), served with H.M. Forces 1914/18
(Major Rifle Brigade). Author of 'Notes on the*

collecting of Incunabula', 'The Murderer's Vade-Mecum', etc.
Recreations: Criminology; bibliophily; music; cricket. Clubs. Marlborough, Egotists. Residence 110A Piccadilly, W. Bredon Hall, Duke's Denver, Norfolk. Arms: Sable, 3 mice courant, argent; crest: a domestic cat crouched as to spring, proper; Motto: 'As my whimsy takes me.'*

Later Wimsey books contain a long biographical note contributed by an unlikely sounding uncle, Paul Austin Delagardie. Although Lord Peter first sprang to prominence in 1923, this disreputable old uncle does not actually appear until 1938, most of his life, if we are to believe him, having been taken up with things French. Mr. Delagardie's contribution to the Wimsey saga is really nothing more than a smoke screen. As Miss Sayers once said the recipe for detective fiction is the art of framing lies. To lead the reader up the garden path and make him believe lies. 'To believe the real murderer to be innocent, to believe some harmless person to be guilty. To believe the false alibi sound, the present absent, the dead alive, the living dead.'†

Although Paul Delagardie may have had a little influence on forming Wimsey's character – teaching

---

* All books.
† *Unpopular Opinions*, p. 185.

him discrimination in wine and suspicion of women – he probably gives himself a great deal more credit than is his due. Miss Sayers has used him to draw so thick a smokescreen, that it is now impossible to identify Wimsey in the way that D.H. Lawrence scholars can seize on a character and cry, 'Ah, that of course is Lady Ottoline Morrell, and this person is quite definitely Peter Warlock.' Mrs. Farren of *Five Red Herrings* weaving away in her Renaissance white woollen dress, could easily be yet another sketch of poor Lady Ottoline. Scarcely any writer of the 1920's had self control enough to leave her out, but who the prototype of Wimsey was remains a mystery. It can be said that he was entirely the writer's creation, but this rarely happens, especially with so well drawn a character as Wimsey. He could be an amalgam of various characters, except for one point: throughout the sixteen or so books, and the many short stories in which he appears, he is absolutely consistent, he never does an un-Wimseylike thing or utters an un-Wimseylike speech. The first hint we have of him is in the first volume of verse published in 1916. It is called *A Man Greatly Gifted* and the subject is likened to an elusive jester. Wimsey was certainly greatly gifted.

He was a respectable scholar in five or six languages, a musician of some skill and more under-

*standing, something of an expert in toxicology, a
collector of rare editions, an entertaining man-
about-town, and a common sensationalist . . . His
passion for the unexplored led him to unravel the
emotional history of Income Tax collectors and to
find out where his own drains led to.**

He could perhaps have been the sad ghost of a lost
war-time lover. Oxford, as everywhere else in the
country, was filled with bereaved women, but it
may have been more noticeable in university towns
when a whole year's intake could be wiped out in
France in less than an hour. The jester simile of the
poem is echoed throughout all the Wimsey books,
becoming rather absurd in *Murder Must Advertise*
when his lordship rushes round the countryside
disguised in a harlequin costume, enticing a wanton
woman to her destruction with a tune played on a
whistle.

The pose, however, of never taking things seri-
ously is just a front which he found difficult to
reconcile with his conscience.

He had taken up criminology as a hobby or, as
we would say nowadays, a therapy to help him over
his ghastly war experiences. He found it exciting
and he enjoyed it – up to a point. When it was clear
that his investigations were likely to lead a man to

* *Clouds of Witness*, p. 71.

12

the scaffold, he despised himself for becoming involved because, unlike the professional policeman, he did not rely on the job for his living. Like all the best detectives in fiction Wimsey was an amateur in the true sense of the word. From the first book to the last he never ceased to have bad dreams about the villains he brought to justice. He shied away from responsibility. As his mother who, in spite of her apparent scattiness understood him very well, said, giving orders for nearly four years to men to go and get blown to pieces 'gives you an inhibition, or an exhibition, or something, of nerves'. Miss Sayers was one of the few detective writers to make her hero follow through the consequences of his work, but fortunately for his peace of mind, not all his villains reached the scaffold. Two of the nicer characters took 'the gentleman's way out'. Penberthy in *Unpleasantness at the Bellona Club* shoots himself as becomes an ex-officer, and Tallboy in *Murder Must Advertise* allows himself to be run over. In *Five Red Herrings* the murder was accidental. In *Unnatural Death* the villainess, quite the nastiest character Miss Sayers created, commits suicide, and the victim is a suicide in *Clouds of Witness*. Miss Sayers does not shrink from detailed descriptions of the state of her victims, but she is sparing of corpses; in only two books are there more than one.

Wimsey's looks and behaviour were meant to give the impression of the typical 'silly ass' of the period. He had straw coloured hair which romantic young ladies saw as gold. A long face, grey eyes and a pointed chin. A prominent nose which nothing could disguise but which proclaimed his aristocratic breeding. He wore his collars high, affected a monocle which was really a powerful magnifying glass and a proceeding which no reputable eye specialist would recommend, particularly in sunny weather. He carried a sword stick marked out in inches, with a compass let in the top. He was short for a romantic character, standing only 5 ft 9 ins., but strong as steel, expert, of course, at ju-jitsu. On only three occasions are we told that he carried a revolver, and only once is it fired but even then only to disarm the villain. He smoked a pipe, cigarettes or cigars as the fancy takes him. His passions are Bach, John Donne and buttered crumpets. We have ample evidence that Miss Sayers herself had a passion for Bach and John Donne, and, as she liked the good things of life, no doubt she had a passion for buttered crumpets too. He drives, at fantastically high speeds, specially built Daimler sports cars, all called Mrs. Merdle. His favourite epithet for his male friends is 'old horse' and his rallying call, 'Come on Steve'. He moves with ease in the highest circles throughout Europe, and English royal personages have been known to bestir themselves on his behalf. He must have moved too in the same orbit as Bertie Wooster, though he preferred the eccentric Egotist Club to the effete Drones. His man Bunter and Jeeves must have frequently met in the Upper Servants' Club and at the various country houses where their employers were guests. But it is doubtful if either the masters or their men were ever really friends. Wimsey, who must have been older than Wooster, had seen the horrors of the First World War, and the gap between those who had and those who had not gone through that holocaust is visible even today among old men in their seventies and eighties. Bunter, although cleverer, would not have been entirely at home with Jeeves, who was no doubt bred to domestic service for as many generations as his master's family had been born to rule him. Bunter, however, was almost certainly a first generation gentleman's gentleman. He had been Wimsey's batman in the war, but his beginnings, if his language is anything to go by, were very common indeed!

Why did Miss Sayers make her hero a lord? Well, she was a middle-class lady and, like many of her generation, romantic. Somerville College produced before, during and after the First World War a large number of outwardly formidable feminists – who nevertheless brought forth many dainty volumes of verse, almost all of them inspired by one theme, the quest of the Holy Grail, King Arthur and his knights, and, as the modern young have it, 'all that jazz'. It was probably a mistake to have placed Wimsey among the English aristocracy 'with sixteen generations of feudal privilege' behind him. Very few English noble families go back that far in the first creation; rebellions and monarchial head choppings have seen to that. In Scotland, as in all other matters, it is different. A lordship there can be lost in the mists of time. This constant supply of new blood is one of the reasons why the English aristocracy is as firmly entrenched today as it ever was. Miss Sayers knew that 'everyone loves a lord' but assumed the wrong reasons. Everyone in England loves a lord, because almost any Englishman can, if he sets his mind to it, become a lord.

Like King Arthur, Wimsey had his knights around him. Bunter, doing all the things it was not proper for a lord to do: ticking off the servants, courting – for information purposes only – housemaids and other female denizens below stairs. Bunter the expert photographer; the follower of suspects – Wimsey was hopeless at disguises – and being nanny when sickness, accident or nightmare plagued his master. He could, when duty called, perform a vulgar comic song at a village concert. But above all, Bunter performed the impossible by staying on when his lordship married. If ever it had come to the stage where Wimsey had to chose between Bunter and Harriet Vane the balance would probably have tipped towards Harriet, so great was his passion and so rigid his ideas of gentlemanly conduct. But the marriage would have been doomed from the start, and we should have missed two of the stories in this book, *The Haunted Policeman* and *Talboys*, which show Wimsey as a married man and father, a state which he embraced rather late in life.

Other characters appear in more than one book. There is Salcombe Hardy – the always sozzled newsman with his 'drowned violets' eyes. A common Fleet Street phenomenon, he does little to further the plots except to start up useful trains of thought. The Hon. Freddy Arbuthnot was almost brainless but he knew all about stocks and shares. This was the age of the Hatry scandals and the papers were filled with reports of dubious financial undertakings. Freddy helped to bring to book the murderer in *Whose Body?*.

Unlike so many fictional detectives, Wimsey had a proper respect for the police. A fool detective, Inspector Sugg, did appear in *Whose Body?* and *Clouds of Witness*, and was telephoned in *Unnatural Death*, but was not heard of thereafter. The painstaking, unsurprisable Inspector Charles Parker – later promoted Chief Inspector – was an admirable foil for the mercurial Wimsey. Parker, who paid a pound a week for rooms in Great Ormond Street, was educated at Barrow-in-Furness Grammar School, and his only hobby was reading Biblical commentaries. If Miss Sayers had only invented Parker and left Wimsey out of things, we should still have a valuable asset in the detective fiction market. For Parker is a fully rounded character. His hobby, which sounds on the surface so outlandish, is in keeping. Any senior policeman who wants to keep sane takes up some kind of hobby remote from his daily round, painting, gliding, violin making, or, like Parker, some esoteric form of scholarship. They usually, however, keep their hobbies very quiet even from their colleagues, so it would seem that Miss Sayers must have got to know the police, or at least one policeman, very well indeed. It was a great convenience to marry Parker to Wimsey's sister, and thus have a Chief Inspector always on tap.

Being a lord, naturally Wimsey would have access to the finest K.C. in the country, Sir Impey Biggs, handsome Member of Parliament and well known canary breeder. And the great pathologist Sir James Lubbock was always accessible to him. One thing all freelance investigators must have is unlimited wealth. The moderns, like Bond, draw on the state or an agency like U.N.C.L.E. Wimsey was wealthy in his own right. He was able, in an age of Depression and slumps to buy whatever he wanted. He could pay Bunter the fantastic wage of £200 a year, an unparalleled sum for an 'all found' situation in 1923. In 1938 he could afford to set up house in the West End with a staff of eight servants besides Bunter and a housekeeper. His money, we are told, did not come from the Denver estates, which were run at a loss, but from London property. Wimsey could not only buy anything, but anybody. He had only to crackle a banknote for hidden files and secrets to be instantly revealed to him and the glint of silver bought him the devotion of small children, char-women, porters and all the lower orders.

It has been said that contemporary fiction gives a better idea of the social life of a period than any learned treatise written in retrospect. Wimsey is now a period piece and if we had no other record of the years 1923–38 than the dozen or so books featuring him, what could we learn from them of that era? It is surprising, taking them altogether, how much social history is, accidentally as it were, packed into them. Oddly enough, much of what we think of today as new, has been about for half a century. This applies both to things and to attitudes. In 1923 Bunter was using a wide angled lens in his photographic work, and travelling on the underground with tickets bought from a machine. The young were spending hours in cafes discussing 'free love, the prurience of prudery, D. H. Lawrence, and the immoral significance of long skirts'.* A character asks 'have you heard Robert Snoates recite his own verse to the tom-tom and pennywhistle?'†

It is unlikely that Miss Sayers heard such a recital; she was satirising the Bloomsbury fringe of the twenties, which has been done, alas all too often. It is amazing what she got away with. Her descriptions of the Chelsea goings-on in *Unpleasantness at the Bellona Club* would have been banned if it had come out in any of D. H. Lawrence's books. This book too brings poignantly back to those of us old enough to remember, the Depression and the terrible disillusion of the young officers who survived the war. We can experience again the cathartic atmosphere of Armistice Day, when the evening papers would nearly always have a horror story: 'Man shouts during Silence' or 'Motorist refuses to turn off engine – assaulted by crowd.' And the next day's picture would always be of a ploughman halted on the headland, cap in hand, head bowed; children round country cenotaphs, royalty round Whitehall's. Two minutes of strange, almost sickening national solidarity, lost forever in the betrayal of the dead by the Second World War.

* *Clouds of Witness*, p. 103.
† *Clouds of Witness*, p. 103.

And there was the ever threatening Red Menace. Almost every book mentions the possibility of a Russian takeover plot – as does almost every detective book published today. Something else which has scarcely moved an inch, oddly enough, is advertising.

> *Tell England. Tell the world. Eat more oats. Take care of your complexion. Shine your shoes with Shino. Ask your Grocer – Children love Laxamalt. Bung's Beer is Better. Try Dogsbody's Sausages. Give them Crunchlets. Stop that sneeze with Snuffo. Flush your kidneys with Fizzlets. Flush your drains with Sanfect.*

This could be a selection of television trailers for the advertising spot instead of the concluding paragraph of *Murder Must Advertise* published in 1933. Wimsey who had been taken on the staff of Pym's agency to find the murderer considered the job immoral. 'We spend our whole time asking intimate questions of perfect strangers "Mother, has your child learnt regular habits?" "Are you *sure* your toilet paper is germ free?" "Do you ever ask yourself about Body Odour?" Upon my soul I sometimes wonder why the long suffering public doesn't rise up and slay us.'*

* *Murder Must Advertise*, p. 50.

They did not in 1933, and they do not now. Incidentally one of Pym's agency's most successful campaigns was headlined 'If you kept a cow in your kitchen'. This banner is used in reality today to advertise powdered milk on television.

It is always a literary argument as to how much of herself an author puts into her work. Dorothy L. Sayers was, as I have said, an intellectual woman with a passion for poetry. She gave this passion to her hero who is never at a loss for an apt quotation. Some of the books have verses as chapter headings. To many critics, her habit of quotations, not only in English but in French, Latin and Greek as well, is sheer intellectual snobbery. It is possible she could not help it and, as Wimsey says, a quotation 'saves original thinking'. She makes no concession to the lesser mind, Wimsey and Harriet Vane telegraph each other in Latin and make love in French (Miss Sayers does not deign to translate). The clue to the whole plot of *Clouds of Witness* is contained in a three page letter in French and one feels that the English version which follows is only supplied at the insistence of the publisher. But if such things annoy the reviewer who has not had the advantage of a university education, surely it is flattering to the reader. It assumes he is as clever as the author, and apart from the instance quoted above, the quotations in no way detract from the flow of the detective story. . . . If Miss Sayers had a weakness it was in depicting what she shamelessly calls 'the lower orders'. All the workmen misplace their aitches or talk like Walter Gabriels, but then Walter Gabriel is still at it. Also, in the context of present day thought, some of her remarks about 'Jewboys' and 'niggers' are hard to take. No one today would dare to write dialogue for a policeman which she writes in the second story of this book, although no one can deny, more now, probably, than then, such sentiments might be expressed.

Wimsey himself is not supposed to be a snob. One of his angriest moments is when a man 'drove me to the indescribable vulgarity of reminding him who I was'. It is always emphasised that for a rich man he is extremely thoughtful, not accepting an invitation to supper, for instance because he knew the couple couldn't afford it, and although he would have accepted Bunter's last drop of blood as of right, he would have remembered to say 'thank you' for it. For a woman with her gifts those years in an advertising agency would probably have been purgatory if she had not found some release in writing, and lavishing on her hero all those things she did not possess. But why detective fiction? Why not romance or historical novels? She probably knew history too well to turn it into fiction, and though romance does come into Wimsey it is never an overriding feature because at the time detective stories sold better than any other kind of book. So that is what she wrote. The bare bones of her detection, the laying of clue on clue leading to a logical climax has scarcely ever been better done. Her trouble was, so many of her critics considered, she would go off into unnecessary by-ways and not keep her villain secret until the end. About this she says, when discussing *Five Red Herrings*:

'I quite appreciate the point you make about the decline of the "pure puzzle story" but I wanted to try my hand at just one of that kind. I am always afraid of getting into a rut. I have been annoyed (stupidly enough) by a lot of reviewers who observed that in my last book I had lost my grip, because the identity of the murderer was obvious from the start (as indeed it is also in *Unnatural Death* and *The Documents in the Case*). Personally, I feel that it is only when the identity of the murderer *is* obvious that the reader can really concentrate on the question (much the most interesting): *how* did he do it? But if people really want to play "spot the murderer" I don't mind obliging them – for once! They have also grumbled that Lord Peter (a) falls in love (b) talks too discursively. Here is a book in which nobody falls in love (unless you count Campbell) and in which practically every sentence is necessary to the plot. . . . Much good may it do 'em!"*

What with obtuse reviewers, earning her living at a job she did very well but in her heart despised, and hating the kind of Press publicity her writing brought, it is no wonder she sometimes lost her temper, and wrote furiously to Victor Gollancz for advertising her book without the middle initial, 'L', in her name.

It is unlikely that she set out with the intention of teaching through detection, but one can learn a great deal from her books. They practically all deal with a specialised subject needing meticulous research. The first Wimsey book *Whose Body?* (1923) is a short straightforward whodunit in which the victim is clubbed and dissected. But from then on the stories become longer and more involved, and as Wimsey grows older his habit of quoting poetry becomes more pronounced. In *Unnatural Death* (1927) the method of murder is simple and almost untraceable. I suspect it is not so easy as it appears to be, although it is horribly reminiscent of the way the Nazis disposed of some of their victims.

* Unpublished letter to Victor Gollancz.

This is one of the few stories in which there is more than one victim. Of *Five Red Herrings* (1931) Miss Sayers says, 'All the places are real places, and all the trains real trains.' She must have spent a great deal of time walking around Kirkcudbright, making endless enquiries of railway staff and checking time tables. This book is of interest to the growing number of people who have a passion for old railway systems, as well as to fans of Wimsey. This, I think, is what makes Dorothy L. Sayers' work so popular. The books can be read by people who have special interests apart from a liking for detective fiction. Take for instance *Murder Must Advertise* (1933). Here we have the authentic setting which she knew so well, the advertising agency. Apart from the story, it lifts the lid off the promotion business in spite of the author's note at the beginning of the book, 'I don't suppose there is a more harmless and law abiding set of people in the world than the advertising experts of Great Britain. The idea that any crime could possibly be perpetrated on Advertising premises is one that could only occur to the ill-regulated fancy of a detective novelist trained to fasten the guilt upon the Most Unlikely Person.' One cannot help feeling that this was her intention, for throughout the book she says very little in praise of advertising. She is, incidentally, supposed to have invented the slogan, 'It pays to advertise.'

Where the solution to a plot depended on accurate timing, she would check this herself over and over again. In the case of *Murder Must Advertise* this involved her and a friend rushing up and down the iron back staircase of Benson's after office hours. Miss Sayers was a somewhat large lady (she has been likened to a 'refined elephant' by one writer, and to 'an eighteenth century admiral, with a kind of Rowlandson jollity about her', by another) so this task cannot have been easy.

Wimsey is always 'trying to be funny' – and quite often he is. There is a vein of humour running through most of the books and in some cases, particularly in *Gaudy Night* (1935) there are scenes which are probably funnier now than they seemed when the books were first published.

Gaudy Night is set in a women's college at Oxford – again a venue Dorothy L. Sayers knew very well – and although it is a true mystery story, there is no murder, although one is attempted. The scene at a literary party is timeless; there is much backbiting chat about a recently published prize-winning novel called 'Mock Turtle' of which one of the guests gives a summary.

It's about this swimming instructor at a watering place, who contracts such an unfortunate anti-nudity complex through watching so many bath-

*ing beauties that it completely inhibits his natural
emotions. So he gets on a whaler and falls in love
at first sight with an Eskimo because she's such a
beautiful bundle of garments. So he marries her
and brings her back to live in a suburb, where she
falls in love with a vegetarian nudist. So then the
husband goes slightly mad and contracts a complex about giant turtles, and spends all his time
staring into the turtle tank at the Aquarium. I
think significant is the word that describes the
book. Yes, significant.**

Miss Sayers no doubt thought she was concocting
utter nonsense, but that is the kind of book which is
often published nowadays, and which wins literary
prizes! The whole party scene has little to do with
the plot – but it puts the characters in their right
setting.

Gaudy Night also contains some highly charged
love scenes between Wimsey and Harriet Vane.
They first met in *Strong Poison* (1930) when Harriet was tried and convicted for the murder of her
lover. In the short time left between the verdict and
the time of execution Wimsey has to discover the
real murderer and prove Harriet's innocence. He
falls hopelessly in love with her, but through several
books Harriet keeps him at bay because she believes

* *Gaudy Night.*

she is under no obligation to him and that he is sorry for her. He wins her at last in *Gaudy Night*. Like all Miss Sayers' heroines she has a weird taste in dress, being married in gold *lamé*, which seems a bit much for a bride past her first youth. Throughout the chronicle it is obvious that Wimsey is adept in the arts of love, but his affairs are only mentioned in passing. There was the youthful folly of Barbara, vaguely referred to by Wimsey, and related more fully by his uncle. There were hints about a Viennese opera singer, and the assumption is that a close relationship had once existed, outside the books, with the artist Marjorie Phelps, who appears in *Unpleasantness at the Bellona Club* and *Strong Poison*. It was not until he was 45 that Wimsey gained his 'America, his new found land' in Harriet.

The *Nine Tailors* (1934) is generally regarded as the best of all Wimsey stories. The setting is the wild Fens of snow and flood, and the plot is woven round the art of campanology (a word which this book brought into general use) which is the complex science of bell ringing and is peculiarly English. In her forward to the book Miss Sayers asks 'the indulgence of all change ringers for any errors I may have made in dealing with their ancient craft'. Although a pedantic clergyman claims to have found Miss Sayers in error 36 times, whatever these may be they do not detract from the story and one does at least learn a great deal about an art which might have passed one by. I know of at least two young people who were inspired to take up bell ringing solely through reading *Nine Tailors*.

The last full length Wimsey book appeared in 1938, but he continued for many years in short stories. The art of short story writing is quite different from that of writing long novels, and short detective stories particularly difficult. The crime, the unravelling and denoument has to be crammed into about 10,000 words at the most, whereas with a novel it is possible to roam through any number. Considering the discursiveness of some of the Wimsey books, it might have been thought impossible to confine him in such a narrow compass, but without losing any of his character or mannerisms Miss Sayers manages to do this admirably. We lose Bunter almost entirely (he has to be content with a message or a telephone call); and Chief Inspector Parker makes few appearances. Some of the short stories are as macabre and horrific as the modern trend could wish. Ian Fleming's *Goldfinger* merely covered people with gold paint, but in *The Abominable History of the Man With Copper Fingers* the villain electro plated his victims and made one of them into an art deco chaiselongue. This story contains some useful hints on copper plating which shows that even for a short story Miss Sayers took a great deal of trouble with her research. For sheer nastiness *The Piscatorial Farce of the Stolen Stomach* is unbeatable.

Many of her short stories do not concern either Wimsey or Montague Egg and are not always detective stories. Some are exercises in Gothic horror, such as *Scrawns* which is Miss Sayers taking the micky out of the Frankenstein cult. *The Cyprian Cat* is very sinister indeed.

The first story in this book *Striding Folly* is more a horror story than detection. The other two are positively the last glimpses of Wimsey. First as a new father in *The Haunted Policeman*; and then as a mature married man with three bouncing sons keeping his hand in with an investigation into stolen fruit. Both stories contain some very sensible remarks on child care!

Looking back over the Wimsey saga is like reviewing the life of an old friend. His character deepened as time went on. He had his failings, but the reason why he has kept his place in our affections is that he was not only Miss Sayers' ideal, but our ideal too of 'the perfect English gentleman' (an ideal that goes back to Chaucer and his 'parfait gentil knight'). He suffered a slight eclipse in the rough, tough fifties and early sixties when good manners, correct speech and any kind of 'graciousness' in the true sense of the word, were looked upon, not only as 'old hat' but positively bad. Now, I detect, in spite of what we read in the press and see on the television, a return to the more Wimsey-like virtues. It was held a few years ago that all readers wanted to know about was people like themselves, so-called 'real' people, as if the inhabitants of *Coronation Street* and Alf Garnett were more 'real' than a member of the House of Lords. They all exist and are therefore all 'real'.

As another lady novelist, Ouida, wrote in the 1890's: 'Realism! The dome of St. Peter's is as real as the gasometer of East London, the passion flower is as real as the potato. I do not object to realism in fiction; what I object to is the limitation of realism in fiction to what is commonplace, tedious and bald.' To which Miss Sayers would no doubt have added 'Hear! Hear!'

Wimsey has survived, and will continue to survive, because he is well written, beautifully constructed, and above all, amusing. He was, to begin with, not only a modern King Arthur, but in a way Miss Sayers' dream of herself. He had all her tastes, did all the things she longed to do and had all the money she did not possess. When, through him, she did get the money, she was glad to have done with him.

People who knew Miss Sayers speak of her jollity (where are the *jolly* ladies of today?) and kindness, of her great good humour and ability to laugh at herself. Both men and women found her excellent company. She never mastered the art of clothing well her tall figure. In the early days when money was short she made her own black dresses ('it doesn't show the dirt') cut on a medieval pattern. In later years her clothes were expensive but, as someone described them, 'obsolete'. Wimsey is a great food enthusiast and so was his creator. When she could afford good food she was quite unable to resist it, and in her later years put on rather too much weight. But these are only superficial things; we know little of the real Dorothy L. Sayers, for she guarded her private life like a tigress, always refusing interviews or requests for memoirs. Again she would no doubt have agreed with Ouida who thought memoirs 'a base betrayal of others, and show great vanity in the writers. To possess any interest they must be treacheries – in general to the dead who cannot defend themselves.' No one could accuse Dorothy L. Sayers of this kind of treachery. In 1926 she married Captain Atherton Fleming – a shattered war hero – and cared for him with love and infinite patience until his death in 1950. Wimsey's war-tormented dreams were no doubt his, but we cannot know for sure. Her faith was strong, and much of her later writings and broadcasting work was on theological themes. But she was not ritualistic, she had no room for form and ceremony for its own sake. 'Perhaps if the churches had had the courage to lay their emphasis where Christ laid it, we might not have come to this frame of mind in which it is assumed that the value of all work, and the value of all people, is to be assessed in terms of economics,' she wrote in an essay called *Christian Morality*.* The young ladies of today, when they've run out of ammunition in their war against men should recharge their magazines from another of her essays *The-Human-Not-Quite-Human*.

She was a member of the Detection Club and edited a number of volumes of detective stories. She was always anxious to stress the difference between being a writer of detection, and a crime and thriller writer. The one is the solving of a puzzle, in which no violence need occur – indeed there is no violence in the two Wimsey stories in this book; the other cannot exist without murder, or at any rate some kind of violent crime. As Miss Sayers says, detective fiction is the art of framing lies . . . 'but mark! of framing lies in the *right way*. There is the crux. Any fool can tell a lie, and any fool can believe it; but the right method is to tell the *truth* in such a way that the *intelligent* reader is seduced into telling a lie for himself. That the writer himself should tell a flat lie is contrary to all the canons of detective art.' It is

* *Unpopular Opinions*. Originally.

34

this phrase 'the *intelligent* reader' that might cut Miss Sayers off from some people. One criticism of her work was that it was only written for people with high-grade brains. That her readership is so wide would seem to refute this criticism. It is more likely that Miss Sayers assumed that all her readers were intelligent, which is not quite the same thing as writing only for the very bright.

She began her writing career as a poet, and even the most frivolous of her tales contains poetic imagery. *Below in the cool cellar, lie row upon row of dusty bottles, each an enchanted glass coffin in which the Sleeping Beauty of the wine grows ever more ravishing in sleep* is one. *He walked in and out of her mind as if it was his own flat* is another.

The Man Born to be King which caused such a furore when it was first broadcast in 1941–42 because it set Christ in an 'ordinary' world using the language of today, stirred not a ripple when it was re-broadcast two or three years ago. Some classical scholars do not think a great deal of Dorothy L. Sayers' Dante translations, probably because she has made Dante so easy to read and understand. These two works would appear to contradict the theory that she wrote only for other intellectuals. She considered that all great literature should be available to everyone not just to the classical few.

But the bells of Fenchurch St. Paul's in *Nine Tailors* with Lord Peter ringing at No. 2 will last as long as people read:

The bells gave tongue: Gaude, Sabaoth, John, Jericho, Jubilee, Dimity, Batty Thomas and Tailor Paul, rioting and exulting high up in the dark tower, wide mouths rising and falling, brazen tongues clamouring, huge wheels turning to the dance of the leaping ropes. Tin tan dan din bo bim bom . . . every bell in her place striking tuneably, hunting up, hunting down, dodging, snapping, laying her blows behind, making her thirds and fourths, working down to lead the dance again. Out over the flat white wastes of fen, over the spear-straight steel dark dykes and the wind bent groaning poplar trees, bursting from the snow-choked louvres of the belfry, whirled away southward and westward in gusty blasts of clamour to the sleeping counties went the music of the bells – little Gaude, silver Sabaoth, strong John and Jericho, glad Jubilee, sweet Dimity and old Batty Thomas, with great Tailor Paul bawling and striding like a giant in the midst of them. Up and down went the shadows of the ringers on the walls, up and down went the scarlet sallies, roofwards and floorwards, and up and down hunting in their courses, went the bells of Fenchurch St. Paul.

Very nice, you might say, but what has all this to do with solving the mystery of a faceless and handless corpse in a grave belonging to someone else?

Well that's just it, it has everything to do with it.

Janet Hitchman
1972

Striding Folly

A LORD PETER WIMSEY STORY

Lord Peter

'Shall I expect you next Wednesday for our game as usual?' asked Mr Mellilow.

'Of course, of course,' replied Mr Creech. 'Very glad there's no ill feeling, Mellilow. Next Wednesday as usual. Unless . . .' his heavy face darkened for a moment, as though at some disagreeable recollection. 'There may be a man coming to see me. If I'm not here by nine, don't expect me. In that case, I'll come on Thursday.'

Mr Mellilow let his visitor out through the french window and watched him cross the lawn to the wicket gate leading to the Hall grounds. It was a clear October night, with a gibbous moon going down the sky. Mr Mellilow slipped on his goloshes (for he was careful of his health and the grass was wet) and himself went down past the sundial and the fish-pond and through the sunk garden till he came to the fence that bounded his tiny freehold on the southern side. He leaned his arms on the rail and gazed across the little valley at the tumbling river and the wide slope beyond, which was crowned, at a mile's distance, by the ridiculous stone tower known as the Folly. The valley, the slope and the tower all belonged to Striding Hall. They lay there, peaceful and lovely in the moonlight, as though nothing could ever disturb their fantastic solitude. But Mr Mellilow knew better.

He had bought the cottage to end his days in, thinking that here was a corner of England the same yesterday, today and for ever. It was strange that he, a chess-player, should not have been able to see three moves ahead. The first move had been the death of the old squire. The second had been the purchase by Creech of the whole Striding property. Even then, he had not been able to see why a rich business man – unmarried and with no rural interests – should have come to live in a spot so remote. True, there were three considerable towns at a few miles' distance, but the village itself was on the road to nowhere. Fool! he had forgotten the Grid! It had come, like a great, ugly chess-rook swooping from an unconsidered corner, marching over the country, straddling four, six, eight parishes at a time, planting hideous pylons to mark its progress, and squatting now at Mr Mellilow's very door. For Creech had just calmly announced that he was selling the valley to the Electrical Company; and there would be a huge power-plant on the river and workmen's bungalows on the slope, and then Development – which, to Mr Mellilow, was another name for the devil. It was ironical that Mr Mellilow, alone in the village, had received Creech with kindness, excusing his vulgar humour and insensitive manners, because he thought Creech was lonely and believed him to be well-meaning, and because he was glad to have a neighbour who could give him a weekly game of chess.

Mr Mellilow came in sorrowful and restored his goloshes to their usual resting-place on the verandah by the french window. He put the chessmen away and the cat out and locked up the cottage – for he lived quite alone, with a woman coming in by the day. Then he went up to bed with his mind full of the Folly, and presently he fell asleep and dreamed.

He was standing in a landscape whose style seemed very familiar to him. There was a wide plain, intersected with hedgerows, and crossed in the middle distance by a river, over which was a small stone bridge. Enormous blue-black thunder-clouds hung heavy overhead, and the air had the electric stillness of something stretched to snapping point. Far off, beyond the river, a livid streak of sunlight pierced the clouds and lit up with theatrical brilliance a tall, solitary tower. The scene had a curious unreality, as though of painted canvas. It was a picture, and he had an odd conviction that he recognised the handling and could put a name to the artist. 'Smooth and tight,' were the words that occurred to him. And then: 'It's bound to break before long.' And then: 'I ought not to have come out without my goloshes.'

It was important, it was imperative that he should get to the bridge. But the faster he walked, the greater the distance grew, and without his goloshes the going was very difficult. Sometimes he was bogged to the knee, sometimes he floundered on steep banks of shifting shale; and the air was not merely oppressive – it was *hot* like the inside of an oven. He was running now, with the breath labouring in his throat, and when he looked up he was astonished to see how close he was to the tower. The bridge was fantastically small now, dwindled to a pin-point on the horizon, but the tower fronted him just across the river, and close on his right was a dark wood, which had not been there before. Something flickered on the wood's edge, out and in again,

shy and swift as a rabbit; and now the wood was between him and the bridge and the tower behind it, still glowing in that unnatural streak of sunlight. He was at the river's brink, but the bridge was nowhere to be seen – and the tower, the tower was moving. It had crossed the river. It had taken the wood in one gigantic leap. It was no more than fifty yards off, immensely high, shining, and painted. Even as he ran, dodging and twisting, it took another field in its stride, and when he turned to flee it was there before him. It was a double tower – twin towers – a tower and its mirror image, advancing with a swift and awful stealth from either side to crush him. He was pinned now between them, panting. He saw their smooth, yellow sides tapering up to heaven, and about their feet went a monstrous stir, like the quiver of a crouching cat. Then the low sky burst like a sluice and through the drench of the rain he leapt at a doorway in the foot of the tower before him and found himself climbing the familiar stair of Striding Folly. 'My goloshes will be here,' he said, with a passionate sense of relief. The lightning stabbed suddenly through a loop-hole and he saw a black crow lying dead upon the stairs. Then thunder . . . like the rolling of drums.

The daily woman was hammering upon the door. 'You *have* slept in,' she said, 'and no mistake.'

*　　*　　*

Mr Mellilow, finishing his supper on the following
Wednesday, rather hoped that Mr Creech would
not come. He had thought a good deal during the
week about the electric percolator, and the more
he thought about it, the less he liked it. He had
discovered another thing which interested his
Gailke, Sir Henry Hunter had a good deal
of it and on the other side had, it
appeared, offered the
thing in every
a choice of

the death
optimis
like death, he w
the building, I hope he
breaks his damned neck one of these days, said the
bitterly.

Mr Mellilow was and he like
to hear their crooked transactions, but as men,
he supposed, were like that; but if they were, he
would rather not play games with them. It spoilt
things, somehow, better, perhaps, not to think too

Mr Mellilow, finishing his supper on the following Wednesday, rather hoped that Mr Creech would not come. He had thought a good deal during the week about the electric power scheme, and the more he thought about it, the less he liked it. He had discovered another thing which had increased his dislike. Sir Henry Hunter, who owned a good deal of land on the other side of the market town, had, it appeared, offered the Company a site more suitable than Striding in every way on extremely favourable terms. The choice of Striding seemed inexplicable, unless on the supposition that Creech had bribed the surveyor. Sir Henry voiced his suspicions without any mincing of words. He admitted, however, that he could prove nothing. 'But he's crooked,' he said; 'I have heard things about him in Town. Other things. Ugly rumours.' Mr Mellilow suggested that the deal might not, after all, go through. 'You're an optimist,' said Sir Henry. 'Nothing stops a fellow like Creech. Except death. He's a man with enemies . . .' He broke off, adding, darkly, 'Let's hope he breaks his damned neck one of these days – and the sooner the better.'

Mr Mellilow was uncomfortable. He did not like to hear about crooked transactions. Business men, he supposed, were like that; but if they were, he would rather not play games with them. It spoilt things, somehow. Better, perhaps, not to think too much about it. He took up the newspaper, determined to occupy his mind, while waiting for Creech, with that day's chess problem. White to play and mate in three.

He had just become pleasantly absorbed when a knock came at the door front. Creech? As early as eight o'clock? Surely not. And in any case, he would have come by the lawn and the french window. But who else would visit the cottage of an evening? Rather disconcerted, he rose to let the visitor in. But the man who stood on the threshold was a stranger.

'Mr Mellilow?'

'Yes, my name is Mellilow. What can I do for you?'

(A motorist, he supposed, inquiring his way or wanting to borrow something.)

'Ah! that is good. I have come to play chess with you.'

'To play chess?' repeated Mr Mellilow, astonished.

'Yes; I am a commercial traveller. My car has broken down in the village. I have to stay at the inn and I ask the good Potts if there is anyone who can give me a game of chess to pass the evening. He tells me Mr Mellilow lives here and plays well. Indeed, I recognise the name. Have I not read *Mellilow on Pawn-Play*? It is yours, no?'

Rather flattered, Mr Mellilow admitted the authorship of this little work.

'So. I congratulate you. And you will do me the favour to play with me, hey? Unless I intrude, or you have company.'

'No.' said Mr Mellilow. 'I am more or less expecting a friend, but he won't turn up till nine and perhaps he won't come at all.'

'If he come, I go,' said the stranger. 'It is very good of you.' He had somehow oozed his way into the house without any direct invitation and was removing his hat and overcoat. He was a big man with a short, thick curly beard and tinted spectacles, and he spoke in a deep voice with a slight foreign accent. 'My name,' he added, 'is Moses. I represent Messrs. Cohen & Gold of Farringdon Street, the manufacturers of electrical fittings.'

He grinned widely, and Mr Mellilow's heart contracted. Such haste seemed almost indecent. Before the site was even taken! He felt an unreasonable resentment against this harmless Jew. Then, he rebuked himself. It was not the man's fault. 'Come in,' he said, with more cordiality in his voice than he really felt, 'I shall be very glad to give you a game.'

'I am very grateful,' said Mr Moses, squeezing his great bulk through into the sitting-room. 'Ha! you are working out the *Record's* two-mover. It is elegant but not profound. You will not take long to break his back. You permit that I disturb?'

Mr Mellilow nodded, and the stranger began to arrange the board for play.

'You have hurt your hand?' inquired Mr Mellilow.

'It is nothing,' replied Mr Moses, turning back the glove he wore and displaying a quantity of sticking-plaster. 'I break my knuckles trying to start the dam' car. She kick me. Bah! a trifle. I wear a glove to protect him. So, we begin?'

'Won't you have something to drink first?'

'No, no, thank you very much. I have refreshed myself already at the inn. Too many drinks are not good. But do not let that prevent you.'

Mr Mellilow helped himself to a modest whisky and soda and sat down to the board. He won the draw and took the white pieces, playing his king's pawn to king's fourth.

'So!' said Mr Moses, as the next few moves and countermoves followed their prescribed course, 'the *gluco piano*, hey? Nothing spectacular. We try the strength. When we know what we have each to meet, then the surprises will begin.'

The first game proceeded cautiously. Whoever Mr Moses might be, he was a sound and intelligent player, not easily stampeded into indiscretions. Twice Mr Mellilow baited a delicate trap; twice, with a broad smile, Mr Moses stepped daintily out between the closing jaws. The third trap was set more carefully. Gradually, and fighting every step of the way, black was forced behind his last defences. Yet another five minutes and Mr Mellilow said gently, 'Check;' adding, 'and mate in four.' Mr Moses nodded. 'That was good.' He glanced at the clock. 'One hour. You give me my revenge, hey? Now we know one another. Now we shall see.'

Mr Mellilow agreed. Ten minutes past nine. Creech would not come now. The pieces were set up again. This time, Mr Moses took white, opening with the difficult and dangerous Steinitz gambit. Within a few minutes Mr Mellilow realised that, up till now, his opponent had been playing with him in a double sense. He experienced that eager and palpitating excitement which attends the process of biting off more than one can chew. By half-past nine, he was definitely on the defensive; at a quarter to ten, he thought he spied a way out; five minutes later, Mr Moses said suddenly: 'It grows late: we must begin to push a little,' and thrust forward a knight, leaving his queen *en prise*.

Mr Mellilow took prompt advantage of the oversight – and became aware, too late, that he was menaced by the advance of a white rook.

Stupid! How had he come to overlook that? There was an answer, of course . . . but he wished the little room were not so hot and that the stranger's eyes were not so inscrutable behind the tinted glasses. If he could manoeuvre his king out of harm's way for the moment and force his pawn through, he had still a chance. The rook moved in upon him as he twisted and dodged; it came swooping and striding over the board, four, six, eight squares at a time; and now the second white rook had darted out from its corner; they were closing in upon him – a double castle, twin castles, a castle and its mirror-image: O God! it was his dream of striding towers, smooth and yellow and painted. Mr Mellilow wiped his forehead.

'Check!' said Mr Moses. And again, 'Check!' And then, 'Checkmate!'

Mr Mellilow pulled himself together. This would never do. His heart was thumping as though he had been running a race. It was ridiculous to be so much overwrought by a game of chess; and if there was one kind of man in the world that he despised, it was a bad loser. The stranger was uttering some polite common-place – he could not tell what – and replacing the pieces in their box.

'I must go now,' said Mr Moses. 'I thank you very much for the pleasure you have so kindly given me . . . Pardon me, you are a little unwell?'

'No, no,' said Mr Mellilow. 'It is the heat of the fire and the lamp. I have enjoyed our games very much. Won't you take anything before you go?'

'No, I thank you. I must be back before the good Potts locks me out. Again, my hearty thanks.'

He grasped Mr Mellilow's hand in his gloved grip and passed out quickly into the hall. In another moment he had seized hat and coat and was gone. His footsteps died away along the cobbled path.

Mr Mellilow returned to the sitting-room. A curious episode; he could scarcely believe that it had really happened. There lay the empty board, the pieces in their box, the *Record* on the old oak chest with a solitary tumbler beside it; he might have dozed off and dreamed the whole thing for all the trace the stranger's visit had left. Certainly the room was very hot. He threw the french window open. A lop-sided moon had risen, chequering the valley and the slope beyond with patches of black and white. High up and distant, the Folly made a pale streak upon the sky. Mr Mellilow thought he would walk down to the bridge to clear his head. He groped in the accustomed corner for his goloshes. They were not there. 'Where on earth has that woman put them?' muttered Mr Mellilow. And he answered himself, irrationally but with complete conviction: 'My goloshes are up at the Folly.'

His feet seemed to move of their own accord. He was through the garden now, walking quickly down the field to the little wooden foot-bridge. His goloshes were at the Folly. It was imperative that he should fetch them back; the smallest delay would be fatal. 'This is ridiculous,' thought Mr Mellilow to himself. 'It is that foolish dream running in my head. Mrs Gibbs must have taken them away to clean them. But while I am here, I may as well go on; the walk will do me good.'

The power of the dream was so strong upon him that he was almost surprised to find the bridge in its accustomed place. He put his hand on the rail and was comforted by the roughness of the untrimmed bark. Half a mile uphill now to the Folly. Its smooth sides shone in the moonlight, and he turned suddenly, expecting to see the double image striding the fields behind him. Nothing so sensational was to be seen, however. He breasted the slope with renewed courage. Now he stood close beneath the tower – and with a little shock he saw that the door at its base stood open.

He stepped inside, and immediately the darkness was all about him like a blanket. He felt with his foot for the stair and groped his way up between the newel and the wall. Now in gloom, now in the gleam of a loophole, the stair seemed to turn endlessly. Then, as his head rose into the pale glimmer of the fourth window, he saw a shapeless blackness sprawled upon the stair. With a sudden dreadful certainty that *this* was what he had come to see, he mounted further and stooped over it. Creech was lying there dead. Close beside the body lay a pair of goloshes. As Mr Mellilow moved to pick them up, something rolled beneath his foot. It was a white chess-rook.

The police surgeon said that Creech had been dead since about nine o'clock. It was proved that at eight-fifty he had set out towards the wicket gate to play chess with Mr Mellilow. And in the morning light the prints of Mr Mellilow's goloshes were clear, leading down the gravelled path on the far side of the lawn, past the sun-dial and the fish-pond and through the sunk garden and so over the muddy field and the footbridge and up the slope to the Folly. Deep foot-prints they were and close to-gether, such as a man might make who carried a monstrous burden. A good mile to the Folly and half of it uphill. The doctor looked inquiringly at Mr Mellilow's spare form.

'Oh, yes,' said Mr Mellilow. 'I could have carried him. It's a matter of knack, not strength. You see—' he blushed faintly, 'I'm not really a gentleman. My father was a miller and I spent my whole boyhood carrying sacks. Only I was always fond of my books, and so I managed to educate myself and earn a little money. It would be silly to pretend I couldn't have carried Creech. But I didn't do it, of course.'

'It's unfortunate,' said the superintendent, 'that we can't find no trace of this man Moses.' His voice was the most unpleasant Mr Mellilow had ever heard – a sceptical voice with an edge like a saw. 'He never come down to the Feathers, that's a certainty. Potts never set eyes on him, let alone sent him up here with a tale about chess. Nor nobody saw no car neither. An odd gentleman this Mr Moses seems to have been. No footmarks to the front door? Well, it's cobbles, so you wouldn't expect none. That his glass of whisky by any chance, sir? . . . Oh? he wouldn't have a drink, wouldn't he? Ah! And you played two games of chess in this very room? Ah! very absorbing pursoot, so I'm told. You didn't hear poor Mr Creech come up the garden?'

'The windows were shut,' said Mr Mellilow, 'and the curtains drawn. And Mr Creech always walked straight over the grass from the wicket gate.'

'H'm!' said the superintendent. 'So he come, or somebody come, right up on to the verandah and sneaks a pair of goloshes; and you and this Mr Moses are so occupied you don't hear nothing.'

'Come, Superintendent,' said the Chief Constable, who was sitting on Mr Mellilow's oak chest and looked rather uncomfortable. 'I don't think that's impossible. The man might have worn tennis-shoes or something. How about fingerprints on the chessmen?'

'He wore a glove on his right hand,' said Mr Mellilow, unhappily. 'I can remember that he didn't use his left hand at all – not even when taking a piece.'

'A very remarkable gentleman,' said the superintendent again. 'No fingerprints, no footprints, no drinks, no eyes visible, no features to speak of, pops in and out without leaving no trace – a kind of a vanishing gentleman.' Mr Mellilow made a helpless gesture. 'These the chessmen you was using?' Mr Mellilow nodded, and the superintendent turned the box upside-down upon the board, carefully extending a vast enclosing paw to keep the pieces from rolling away. 'Let's see. Two big 'uns with crosses on the top and two big 'uns with spikes. Four chaps with split-open 'eads. Four 'orses. Two black 'uns – what d'you call these? Rooks, eh? Look more like churches to me. One white church – rook if you like. What's gone with the other one? Or don't these rook-affairs go in pairs like the rest?'

'They must both be there,' said Mr Mellilow. 'He was using two white rooks in the end-game. He mated me with them . . . I remember . . .'

He remembered only too well. The dream, and the double castle moving to crush him. He watched the superintendent feeling in his pocket and suddenly knew that name of the terror that had flickered in and out of the black wood.

The superintendent set down the white rook that had lain by the corpse at the Folly. Colour, height and weight matched with the rook on the board.

'Staunton men,' said the Chief Constable, 'all of a pattern.'

But the superintendent, with his back to the french window, was watching Mr Mellilow's grey face.

'He must have put it in his pocket,' said Mr Mellilow. 'He cleared the pieces away at the end of the game.'

'But he couldn't have taken it up to Striding Folly,' said the superintendent, 'nor he couldn't have done the murder, by your own account.'

'Is it possible that you carried it up to the Folly yourself,' asked the Chief Constable, 'and dropped it there when you found the body?'

'The gentleman has said that he saw this man Moses put it away,' said the superintendent.

They were watching him now, all of them. Mr Mellilow clasped his head in his hands. His forehead was drenched. 'Something must break soon,' he thought.

Like a thunderclap there came a blow on the

window; the superintendent leapt nearly out of his skin.

'Lord, my lord!' he complained, opening the window and letting a gust of fresh air into the room, 'How you startled me!'

Mr Mellilow gaped. Who was this? His brain wasn't working properly. That friend of the Chief Constable's, of course, who had disappeared somehow during the conversation. Like the bridge in his dream. Disappeared. Gone out of the picture.

'Absorbin' game, detectin',' said the Chief Constable's friend. 'Very much like chess. People come creepin' right up on to the verandah and you never even notice them. In broad daylight, too. Tell me, Mr Mellilow – what made you go up last night to the Folly?'

Mr Mellilow hesitated. This was the point in his story that he had made no attempt to explain. Mr Moses had sounded unlikely enough; a dream about goloshes would sound more unlikely still.

'Come now,' said the Chief Constable's friend, polishing his monocle on his handkerchief and replacing it with an exaggerated lifting of the eyebrows. 'What was it? Woman, woman, lovely woman? Meet me by moonlight and all that kind of thing?'

'Certainly not,' said Mr Mellilow, indignantly. 'I

wanted a breath of fresh—' He stopped, uncertainly. There was something in the other man's childish-foolish face that urged him to speak the reckless truth. 'I had a dream,' he said.

The superintendent shuffled his feet, and the Chief Constable crossed one leg awkwardly over the other.

'Warned of God in a dream,' said the man with the monocle, unexpectedly. 'What did you dream of?' He followed Mr Mellilow's glance at the board. 'Chess?'

'Of two moving castles,' said Mr Mellilow, 'and the dead body of a black crow.'

'A pretty piece of fused and inverted symbolism,' said the other. 'The dead body of a black crow become a dead man with a white rook.'

'But that came afterwards,' said the Chief Constable.

'So did the end-game with the two rooks,' said Mr Mellilow.

'Our friend's memory works both ways,' said the man with the monocle, 'like the White Queen's. She, by the way, could believe as many as six impossible things before breakfast. So can I. Pharaoh tell your dream.'

'Time's getting on, Wimsey,' said the Chief Constable.

'Let time pass,' retorted the other, 'for, as a

63

great chess-player observed, it helps more than reasoning.'

'What player was that?' demanded Mr Mellilow.

'A lady,' said Wimsey, 'who played with living men and mated kings, popes and emperors.'

'Oh,' said Mr Mellilow. 'Well—' he told his tale from the beginning, making no secret of his grudge against Creech and his nightmare fancy of the striding electric pylons. 'I think,' he said, 'that was what gave me the dream.' And he went on to his story of the goloshes, the bridge, the moving towers and death on the stairs at the Folly.

'A damned lucky dream for you,' said Wimsey. 'But I see now why they chose you. Look! it is all clear as daylight. If you had had no dream – if the murderer had been able to come back later and replace your goloshes – if someone else had found the body in the morning with the chess-rook beside it and your tracks leading back and home again, that might have been mate in one move. There are two men to look for, Superintendent. One of them belongs to Creech's household, for he knew that Creech came every Wednesday through the wicket-gate to play chess with you; and he knew that Creech's chessmen and yours were twin sets. The other was a stranger – probably the man whom Creech half-expected to call upon him. One lay in wait for Creech and strangled him near the wicket gate as he arrived; fetched your goloshes from the verandah and carried the body down to the Folly. And the other came here in disguise to hold you in play and give you an alibi that no one could believe. The one man is strong in his hands and strong in the back – a sturdy, stocky man with feet no bigger than yours. The other is a big man, with noticeable eyes and probably clean-shaven, and he plays brilliant chess. Look among Creech's enemies for those two men and ask them where they were between eight o'clock and ten-thirty last night.'

'Why didn't the strangler bring back the goloshes?' asked the Chief Constable.

'Ah!' said Wimsey; 'that was where the plan went wrong. I think he waited up at the Folly to see the light go out in the cottage. He thought it would be too great a risk to come up twice on to the verandah while Mr Mellilow was there.'

'Do you mean,' asked Mr Mellilow, 'that he was there, *in* the Folly, watching me, when I was groping up those black stairs?'

'He may have been,' said Wimsey. 'But probably, when he saw you coming up the slope, he knew that things had gone wrong and fled away in the opposite direction, to the high road that runs behind the Folly. Mr Moses, of course, went, as he came, by the road that passes Mr Mellilow's door, removing his disguise in the nearest convenient place.'

'That's all very well, my lord,' said the superintendent, 'but where's the proof of it?'

'Everywhere,' said Wimsey. 'Go and look at the tracks again. There's one set going outwards in goloshes, deep and short, made when the body was carried down. One, made later, in walking shoes, which is Mr Mellilow's track going outwards towards the Folly. And the third is Mr Mellilow again, coming back, the track of a man running very fast. Two out and only one in. Where is the man who went out and never came back?'

'Yes,' said the superintendent, doggedly. 'But suppose Mr Mellilow made that second lot of tracks himself to put us off the scent, like? I'm not saying he did, mind you, but why couldn't he have?'

'Because,' said Wimsey, 'he had no time. The in-and-out tracks left by the shoes were made *after* the body was carried down. There is no other bridge for three miles on either side, and the river runs waist-deep. It can't be forded; so it must be crossed by the bridge. But at half-past ten, Mr Mellilow was in the Feathers, on *this* side of the river, ringing up the police. It couldn't be done, Super, unless he had wings. The bridge is there to prove it; for the bridge was crossed three times only.'

'The bridge,' said Mr Mellilow, with a great sigh. 'I knew in my dream there was something important about that. I knew I was safe if only I could get to the bridge.'

The Haunted Policeman

A LORD PETER WIMSEY STORY

The Haunted Policeman

'**G**ood god!' said his lordship. 'Did I do that?'
'All the evidence points that way,' replied his wife.

'Then I can only say that I never knew so convincing a body of evidence produce such an inadequate result.'

The nurse appeared to take this reflection personally. She said in a tone of rebuke:

'He's a *beautiful* boy.'

'H'm,' said Peter. He adjusted his eyeglass more carefully. 'Well, you're the expert witness. Hand him over.'

The nurse did so, with a dubious air. She was

relieved to see that this disconcerting parent handled the child competently; as, in a man who was an experienced uncle, was not, after all, so very surprising. Lord Peter sat down gingerly on the edge of the bed.

'Do you feel it's up to standard?' he inquired with some anxiety. 'Of course, *your* workmanship's always sound – but you never know with these collaborate efforts.'

'I think it'll do,' said Harriet, drowsily.

'Good.' He turned abruptly to the nurse. 'All right; we'll keep it. Take it and put it away and tell 'em to invoice it to me. It's a very interesting addition to you, Harriet; but it would have been a hell of a rotten substitute.' His voice wavered a little, for the last twenty-four hours had been trying ones, and he had had the fright of his life.

The doctor, who had been doing something in the other room, entered in time to catch the last words. 'There was never any likelihood of that, you goop,' he said, cheerfully. 'Now, you've seen all there is to be seen, and you'd better run away and play.' He led his charge firmly to the door. 'Go to bed,' he advised him in kindly accents; 'you look all in.'

'I'm all right,' said Peter. 'I haven't been doing anything. And look here—' He stabbed a belligerent finger in the direction of the adjoining room. 'Tell those nurses of yours, if I want to pick my son up, I'll pick him up. If his mother wants to kiss him, she can damn well kiss him. I'll have none of your infernal hygiene in *my* house.'

'Very well,' said the doctor, 'just as you like. Anything for a quiet life. I rather believe in a few healthy germs myself. Builds up resistance. No, thanks, I won't have a drink. I've got to go on to another one, and an alcoholic breath impairs confidence.'

'Another one?' said Peter, aghast.

'One of my hospital mothers. You're not the only fish in the sea by a long chalk. One born every minute.'

'God! what a hell of a world.' They passed down the great curved stair. In the hall a sleepy footman clung, yawning, to his post of duty.

'All right, William,' said Peter. 'Buzz off now; I'll lock up.' He let the doctor out. 'Good-night – and thanks very much, old man. I'm sorry I swore at you.'

'They mostly do,' replied the doctor philosophically. 'Well, bung-ho, Flim. I'll look in again later, just to earn my fee, but I shan't be wanted. You've married into a good tough family, and I congratulate you.'

The car, spluttering and protesting a little after its long wait in the cold, drove off, leaving Peter alone on the doorstep. Now that it was all over and he could go to bed, he felt extraordinarily wakeful. He would have liked to go to a party. He leaned back against the wrought-iron railings and lit a cigarette, staring vaguely into the lamp-lit dusk of the square. It was thus that he saw the policeman.

The blue-uniformed figure came up from the direction of South Audley Street. He too was smoking and he walked, not with the firm tramp of a constable on his beat, but with the hesitating step of a man who has lost his bearings. When he came in sight, he had pushed back his helmet and was rubbing his head in a puzzled manner. Official habit made him look sharply at the bare-headed gentleman in evening dress, abandoned on a doorstep at three in the morning, but since the gentleman appeared to be sober and bore no signs of being about to commit a felony, he averted his gaze and prepared to pass on.

'Morning, officer,' said the gentleman, as he came abreast with him.

'Morning, sir,' said the policeman.

'You're off duty early,' pursued Peter, who wanted somebody to talk to. 'Come in and have a drink.'

This offer re-awakened all the official suspicion. 'Not just now, sir, thank you,' replied the policeman guardedly.

'Yes, now. That's the point.' Peter tossed away his cigarette-end. It described a fiery arc in the air and shot out a little train of sparks as it struck the pavement. 'I've got a son.'

'Oh, ah!' said the policeman, relieved by this innocent confidence. 'Your first, eh?'

'And last, if I know anything about it.'

'That's what my brother says, every time,' said the policeman. 'Never no more, he says. He's got eleven. Well, sir, good luck to it. I see how you're situated, I and thank you kindly, but after what the sergeant said I dunno as I better. Though if I was to die this moment, not a drop 'as passed me lips since me supper beer.'

Peter put his head on one side and considered this.

'The sergeant said you were drunk?'

'He did, sir.'

'And you were not?'

'No, sir. I saw everything just the same as I told him, though what's become of it now is more than I can say. But drunk I was not, sir, no more than you are yourself.'

'Then,' said Peter, 'as Mr Joseph Surface remarked to Lady Teazle, what is troubling you is the consciousness of your own innocence. He insinuated that you had looked on the wine when it was red – you'd better come in and make it so. You'll feel better.'

The policeman hesitated.

'Well, sir, I dunno. Fact is, I've had a bit of a shock.'

'So've I,' said Peter. 'Come in for God's sake and keep me company.'

'Well, sir—' said the policeman again. He mounted the steps slowly.

The logs in the hall chimney were glowing a deep red through their ashes. Peter raked them apart, so that the young flame shot up between them. 'Sit down,' he said; 'I'll be back in a moment.'

The policeman sat down, removed his helmet, and stared about him, trying to remember who occupied the big house at the corner of the square. The engraved coat of arms upon the great silver bowl on the chimney-piece told him nothing, even though it was repeated in colour upon the backs of two tapestried chairs: three white mice skipping upon a black ground. Peter, returning quietly from the shadows beneath the stair, caught him as he traced the outlines with a thick finger.

'A student of heraldry?' he said. 'Seventeenth-century work and not very graceful You're new to this beat, aren't you? My name's Wimsey.'

He put down a tray on the table.

'If you'd rather have beer or whisky, say so. These bottles are only a concession to my mood.'

The policeman eyed the long necks and bulging

silver-wrapped corks with curiosity. 'Champagne?' he said. 'Never tasted it, sir. But I'd like to try the stuff.'

'You'll find it thin,' said Peter, 'but if you drink enough of it, you'll tell me the story of your life.' The cork popped and the wine frothed out into the wide glasses.

'Well!' said the policeman. 'Here's to your good lady, sir, and the new young gentleman. Long life and all the best. A bit in the nature of cider, ain't it, sir?'

'Just a trifle. Give me your opinion after the third glass, if you can put up with it so long. And thanks for your good wishes. You a married man?'

'Not yet, sir. Hoping to be when I get promotion. If only the sergeant – but that's neither here nor there. You been married long, sir, if I may ask.'

'Just over a year.'

'Ah! and do you find it comfortable, sir?'

Peter laughed.

'I've spent the last twenty-four hours wondering why, when I'd had the blazing luck to get on to a perfectly good thing, I should be fool enough to risk the whole show on a damned silly experiment.'

The policeman nodded sympathetically.

'I see what you mean, sir. Seems to me, life's like that. If you don't take risks, you get nowhere. If you do, things may go wrong, and then where are you?

And 'alf the time, when things happen, they happen first, before you can even think about 'em.'

'Quite right,' said Peter, and filled the glasses again. He found the policeman soothing. True to his class and training, he turned naturally in moments of emotion to the company of the common man. Indeed, when the recent domestic crisis had threatened to destroy his nerve, he had headed for the butler's pantry with the swift instinct of the homing pigeon. There, they had treated him with great humanity, and allowed him to clean the silver.

With a mind oddly clarified by champagne and lack of sleep, he watched the constable's reaction to Pol Roger 1926. The first glass had produced a philosophy of life; the second produced a name – Alfred Burt – and a further hint of some mysterious grievance against the station sergeant; the third glass, as prophesied, produced the story.

'You were right, sir' (said the policeman) 'when you spotted I was new to the beat. I only come on it at the beginning of the week, and that accounts for me not being acquainted with you, sir, nor with most of the residents about here. Jessop, now, he knows everybody and so did Pinker – but he's been took off to another division. You'd remember Pinker – big chap, make two o' me, with a sandy moustache. Yes, I thought you would.

'Well, sir, as I was saying, me knowing the district in a general way, but not, so to speak, like the palm o' me 'and, might account for me making a bit of a fool of myself, but it don't account for me seeing what I did see. See it I did, and not drunk nor nothing like it. And as for making a mistake in the number, well, that might happen to anybody. All the same, sir, 13 was the number I see, plain as the nose on your face.'

'You can't put it stronger than that,' said Peter, whose nose was of a kind difficult to overlook.

'You know Merriman's End, sir?'

'I think I do. Isn't it a long cul-de-sac running somewhere at the back of South Audley Street, with a row of houses on one side and a high wall on the other?'

'That's right, sir. Tall, narrow houses they are, all alike, with deep porches and pillars to them.'

'Yes. Like an escape from the worst square in Pimlico. Horrible. Fortunately, I believe the street was never finished, or we should have had another row of the monstrosities on the opposite side. This house is pure eighteenth century. How does it strike you?'

P.C. Burt contemplated the wide hall – the Adam fireplace and panelling with their graceful shallow mouldings, the pedimented doorways, the high round-headed window lighting hall and gallery, the noble proportions of the stair. He sought for a phrase.

'It's a gentleman's house,' he pronounced at length. 'Room to breathe, if you see what I mean. Seems like you couldn't act vulgar in it.' He shook his head. 'Mind you, I wouldn't call it cosy. It ain't the place I'd choose to sit down to a kipper in me shirtsleeves. But it's got class. I never thought about it before, but now you mention it I see what's wrong with them other houses in Merriman's End. They're sort of squeezed-like. I been into more'n one o' them tonight, and that's what they are; they're squeezed. But I was going to tell you about that.'

'Just upon midnight it was' (pursued the policeman) 'when I turns into Merriman's End in the ordinary course of my dooties. I'd got pretty near down toward the far end, when I see a fellow lurking about in a suspicious way under the wall. There's back gates there, you know, sir, leading into some gardens, and this chap was hanging about inside one of the gateways. A rough-looking fellow, in a baggy old coat – might a' been a tramp off the Embankment. I turned my light on him – that street's not very well lit, and it's a dark night – but I couldn't see much of his face, because he had on a ragged old hat and a big scarf round his neck. I thought he was up to no good, and I was just about to ask him what he was doing there, when I hear a

most awful yell come out o' one o' them houses opposite. Ghastly it was, sir. "Help!" it said. "Murder! help!", fit to freeze your marrow.'

'Man's voice or woman's?'

'Man's, sir. I think. More of a roaring kind of yell, if you take my meaning. I says, "Hullo! What's up there? Which house is it?" The chap says nothing, but he points, and him and me runs across together. Just as we gets to the house, there's a noise like as if someone was being strangled just inside, and a thump, as it might be something falling against the door.'

'Good God!' said Peter.

'I gives a shout and rings the bell. "Hoy!" I says. "What's up here?" and then I knocked on the door. There's no answer, so I rings and knocks again. Then the chap who was with me, he pushed open the letter-flap and squints through it.'

'Was there a light in the house?'

'It was all dark, sir, except the fanlight over the door. That was lit up bright, and when I looks up, I see the number of the house – number 13, painted plain as you like on the transom. Well, this chap peers in, and all of a sudden he gives a kind of gurgle and falls back. "Here!" I says, "what's amiss? Let me have a look." So I puts me eye to the flap and I looks in.'

P.C. Burt paused and drew a long breath. Peter cut the wire of the second bottle.

'Now, sir,' said the policeman, 'believe me or believe me not, I was as sober at that moment as I am now. I can tell you everything I see in that house, same as if it was wrote up there on that wall. Not as it was a great lot, because the flap wasn't all that wide but by squinnying a bit, I could make shift to see right across the hall and a piece on both sides and part way up the stairs. And here's what I see, and you take notice of every word, on account of what come after.'

He took another gulp of the Pol Roger to loosen his tongue and continued:

'There was the floor of the hall. I could see that very plain. All black and white squares it was, like marble, and it stretched back a good long way. About half-way along, on the left, was the staircase, with a red carpet, and the figure of a white naked woman at the foot, carrying a big pot of blue and yellow flowers. In the wall next the stairs there was an open door, and a room all lit up. I could just see the end of a table, with a lot of glass and silver on it. Between that door and the front door there was a big black cabinet, shiny, with gold figures painted on it, like them things they had at the Exhibition. Right at the back of the hall there was a place like a conservatory, but I couldn't see what was in it, only it looked very gay. There was a door on the right, and that was open, too. A very pretty drawing-room, by

what I could see of it, with pale blue paper and pictures on the walls. There were pictures in the hall, too, and a table on the right with a copper bowl, like as it might be for visitors' cards to be put in. Now, I see all that, sir, and I put it to you, if it hadn't a' been there, how could I describe so plain?'

'I have know people describe what wasn't there,' said Peter thoughtfully, 'but it was seldom anything of that kind. Rats, cats and snakes I have heard of, and occasionally naked female figures; but delirious lacquer cabinets and hall-tables are new to me.'

'As you say, sir,' agreed the policeman, 'and I see you believe me so far. But here's something else, what you mayn't find so easy. There was a man laying in that hall, sir, as sure as I sit here and he was dead. He was a big man and clean-shaven, and he wore evening dress. Somebody had stuck a knife into his throat. I could see the handle of it – it looked like a carving knife, and the blood had run out, all shiny, over the marble squares.'

The policeman looked at Peter, passed his handkerchief over his forehead, and finished the fourth glass of champagne.

'His head was up against the end of the hall table,' he went on, 'and his feet must have been up against the door, but I couldn't see anything quite close to me, because of the bottom of the letter-box. You understand, sir, I was looking through the wire cage of the box, and there was something inside – letters, I suppose that cut off my view downwards. But I see all the rest – in front and a bit of both sides; and it must have been regularly burnt in upon me brain, as they say, for I don't suppose I was looking more than a quarter of a minute or so. Then all the lights went out at once, same as if somebody has turned off the main switch. So I looks round, and I don't mind telling you I felt a bit queer. And *when* I looks round, lo and behold! my bloke in the muffler had hopped it.'

'The devil he had,' said Peter.

'Hopped it,' repeated the policeman, 'and there I was. And just there, sir, is where I made my big mistake, for I thought he couldn't a' got far, and I started off up the street after him. But I couldn't see him, and I couldn't see nobody. All the houses was dark, and it come over me what a sight of funny things may go on, and nobody take a mite o' notice. The way I'd shouted and banged on the door, you'd a' thought it'd a' brought out every soul in the street, not to mention that awful yelling. But there – you may have noticed it yourself, sir. A man may leave his ground-floor windows open, or have his chimney a' fire, and you may make noise enough to wake the dead, trying to draw his attention, and nobody give no heed. He's fast asleep, and the neighbours say, "Blast that row, but, it's no business of mine," and stick their 'eads under the bed-clothes.'

'Yes,' said Peter. 'London's like that.'

'That's right, sir. A village is different. You can't pick up a pin there without somebody coming up to ask where you got it from – but London keeps itself to itself . . . Well, something'll have to be done, I thinks to myself, and I blows me whistle. They heard that all right. Windows started to go up all along the street. That's London, too.'

Peter nodded. 'London will sleep through the last trump. Puddley-in-the-Rut and Doddering-in-the-Dumps will look down their noses and put on virtuous airs. But God, who is never surprised, will say to his angel, "Whistle up 'em, Michael, whistle 'em up; East and West will rise from the dead at the sound of the policeman's whistle".'

'Quite so, sir,' said P.C. Burt; and wondered for the first time whether there might not be something in this champagne stuff after all. He waited for a moment and then resumed:

'Well, it so happened that just when I sounded my whistle, Withers – that's the man on the other beat – was in Audley Square, coming to meet me. You know, sir, we has times for meeting one another, arranged different-like every night; and twelve o'clock in the square was our rendy-voos tonight. So up he comes in, you might say; no time at all, and finds me there, with everyone a' hollering at me from the windows to know what was up. Well, naturally, I didn't want the whole bunch of 'em running out into the street and our man getting away in the crowd, so I just tells 'em there's nothing, only a bit of an accident farther along. And then I see Withers and glad enough I was. We stands there at the top o' the street, and I tells him there's a dead man laying in the hall at Number 13, and it looks to me like murder. "Number 13," he says, "you can't mean Number 13. There ain't no Number 13 in Merriman's End, you fathead; it's all even numbers.' And so it is, sir, for the houses on the other side were never built, so there's no odd numbers at all barrin' Number 1, as is the big house on the corner.

'Well, that give me a bit of a jolt. I wasn't so much put out at not having remembered about the numbers, for as I tell you, I never was on the beat before this week. No; but I knew I'd seen that there number writ up plain as pie on the fanlight, and I didn't see how I could have been mistaken. But when Withers heard the rest of the story, he thought maybe I'd misread it for Number 12. It couldn't be 18, for there's only sixteen houses in the road; nor it couldn't be 16 neither, for I knew it wasn't the end house. But we thought it might be 12 or 10; so away we goes to look.

'We didn't have no difficulty about getting in at Number 12. There was a very pleasant old gentleman came down in his dressing-gown, asking what the disturbance was, and could he be of use. I apologised for disturbing him, and said I was afraid there'd been an accident in one of the houses, and had he heard anything. Of course, the minute he opened the door I could see it wasn't Number 12 we wanted; there was only a little hall with polished boards, and the walls plain panelled – all very bare and neat – and no black cabinet nor naked woman nor nothing. The old gentleman said, yes, his son had heard somebody shouting and knocking a few minutes earlier. He'd got up and put his head out of the window, but couldn't see nothing, but they both thought from the sound it was Number 14 forgotten his latch-key again. So we thanked him very much and went on to Number 14.

'We had a bit of a job to get Number 14 downstairs. A fiery sort of gentleman he was, something in the military way, I thought, but he turned out to be a retired Indian Civil Servant. A dark gentleman, with a big voice, and his servant was dark, too – some sort of a nigger. The gentleman wanted to know what the blazes all this row was about, why a decent citizen wasn't allowed to get his proper sleep. He supposed that young fool at Number 12 was drunk again. Withers had to speak a bit sharp to him; but at last the nigger came down and let us in. Well, we had to apologise once more. The hall was not a bit like – the staircase was on the wrong side, for one thing, and though there was a statue at the foot of it, it was some kind of a heathen idol with a lot of heads and arms, and the walls were covered with all sorts of brass stuff and native goods you know the kind of thing. There was a black-and-white linoleum on the floor, and that was about all there was to it. The servant had soft sort of way with him I didn't half like. He said he slept at the back and had heard nothing till his master rang for him. Then the gentleman came to the top of the stairs and shouted out it was no use disturbing him; the noise came from Number 12 as usual, and if that young man didn't stop his blanky Bohemian goings-on, he'd have the law on his father. I asked if he'd seen anything, and he said, no, he hadn't. Of course, sir, me and that other chap was inside the porch, and you can't see anything what goes on inside those porches from the other houses, because they're filled in at the sides with coloured glass – all the lot of them.'

Lord Peter Wimsey looked at the policeman and then looked at the bottle, as though estimating the alcoholic content of each. With deliberation, he filled both glasses again.

'Well, sir,' said P.C. Burt after refreshing himself,

'by this time Withers was looking at me in rather an old-fashioned manner. However, he said nothing, and we went back to Number 10, where there was two maiden ladies and a hall full of stuffed birds and wallpaper like a florists' catalogue. The one who slept in the front was deaf as a post, and the one who slept at the back hadn't heard nothing. But we got hold of their maids, and the cook said she'd heard the voice calling "Help!" and thought it was in Number 12, and she'd hid her head in the pillow and said her prayers. The housemaid was a sensible girl. She'd looked out when she heard me knocking. She couldn't see anything at first, owing to us being in the porch, but she thought something must be going on, so, not wishing to catch cold, she went back to put on her bedroom slippers. When she got back to the window, she was just in time to see a man running up the road. He went very quick and very silent, as if he had goloshes on, and she could see the ends of his muffler flying out behind him. She saw him run out of the street and turn to the right, and then she heard me coming along after him. Unfortunately her eye being on the man, she didn't notice which porch I came out of. Well, that showed I wasn't inventing the whole story at any rate, because there was my bloke in the muffler. The girl didn't recognise him at all, but that wasn't surprising, because she'd only just entered the old ladies' service. Besides, it wasn't likely the man had anything to do with it, because he was outside with me when the yelling started. My belief is, he was the sort as doesn't care to have his pockets examined too close, and the minute my back was turned he thought he'd be better and more comfortable elsewhere.

'Now there ain't no need' (continued the policeman) 'for me to trouble you, sir, with all them houses what we went into. We made inquiries at the whole lot, from Number 2 to Number 16, and there wasn't one of them had a hall in any ways comfortable to what that chap and I saw through the letter-box. Nor there wasn't a soul in 'em could give us any help more than what we'd had already. You see, sir, though it took me a bit o' time telling, it all went very quick. There was the yells; they didn't last beyond a few seconds or so, and before they was finished, we was across the road and inside the porch. Then there was me shouting and knocking; but I hadn't been long at that afore the chap with me looks through the box. Then I has my look inside, for fifteen seconds it might be, and while I'm doing that, my chap's away up the street. Then I runs after him, and then I blows me whistle. The whole thing might take a minute or a minute and a half, maybe. Not more.

'Well, sir; by the time we'd been into every house

in Merriman's End, I was feeling a bit queer again, I can tell you, and Withers, he was looking queerer. He says to me, "Burt," he says, "is this your idea of a joke? Because if so, the 'Olborn Empire's where you ought to be, not the police force." So I tells him over again, most solemn, what I seen – "and," I says, "if only we could lay hands on that chap in the muffler, he could tell you he seen it, too. And what's more," I says, "do you think I'd risk me job, playing a silly trick like that?" He says, "Well, it beats me," he says, "If I didn't know you was a sober kind of chap, I'd say you was seein' things." "Things?" I says to him, "I see that there corpse a-layin' there with the knife in his neck, and that was enough for me. 'Orrible, he looked, and the blood all over the floor." "Well," he says, 'maybe he wasn't dead after all, and they've cleared him out of the way." "And cleared the house away, too, I suppose," I said to him. So Withers says, in an odd sort o'voice, "You're sure about the house? You wasn't letting your imagination run away with you over naked females and such?" That was a nice thing to say. I said. "No, I wasn't. There's been some monkey business going on in this street and I'm going to get to the bottom of it, if we has to comb-out London for that chap in the muffler." "Yes," says Withers, nasty-like, "it's a pity he cleared off so sudden." "Well," I says, "you can't say I imagined *him*, anyhow, because that there girl saw him, and a mercy she did," I said, "or you'd be saying next I ought to be in Colney Hatch." "Well," he says, "I dunno what you think you're going to do about it. You better ring up the station and ask for instructions."

'Which I did. And Sergeant Jones, he come down himself, and he listens attentive-like to what we both has to say. And then he walks along the street, slowlike, from end to end. And then he comes back and says to me, "Now, Burt," he says, "just you describe that hall to me again, careful." Which I does, same as I described it to your, sir. And he says, "You're sure there was the room on the left of the stairs with the glass and silver on the table; and the room on the right with the pictures in it?" And I says, "Yes, Sergeant, I'm quite sure of that." And Withers says, "Ah!" in a kind of got-you-now voice, if you take my meaning. And the sergeant says, "Now, Burt," he says, "pull yourself together and take a look at these here houses. Don't you see they're all single-fronted? There ain't one on 'em has rooms *both* sides o' the front hall. Look at the windows, you fool," he says.'

Lord Peter poured out the last of the champagne.

'I don't mind telling you, sir' (went on the policeman) 'that I was fair knocked silly to think of me never noticing that! Withers had noticed it all right, and that's what made him think I was drunk or barmy. But I stuck to what I'd seen. I said, there must be two of them houses knocked into one, somewhere, but that didn't work, because we'd been into all of them, and there wasn't no such thing – not without there was one o' them concealed doors like you read about in crook stories. "Well, anyhow," I says to the sergeant, "the yells was real all right, because other people heard 'em. Just you ask, and they'll tell you." So the sergeant says, "Well, Burt, I'll give you every chance." So he knocks up Number 12 again – not wishing to annoy Number 14 any more than he was already – and this time the son comes down. An agreeable gentleman he was, too; not a bit put out. He says, Oh, yes, he'd heard the yells and his father'd heard them too. "Number 14," he says, "that's where the trouble is. A very odd bloke, is Number 14, and I shouldn't be surprised if he beats that unfortunate servant of his. The Englishman abroad, you know! The outposts of Empire and all that kind of thing. They're rough and ready – and then the curry in them parts is bad for the liver." So I was for inquiring at Number 14 again; but the sergeant, he loses patience, and says, "You know quite well," he says, "it ain't Number 14, and in my opinion, Burt, you're either dotty or drunk. You best go home straight away," he says, "and sober up, and I'll see you again when you can give a better account of yourself." So I argues a bit, but it ain't no use, and away he goes, and Withers goes back to his beat. And I walks up and down a bit till Jessop comes to take over, and then I comes away, and that's when I sees you, sir.

'But I ain't drunk, sir – at least, I wasn't then, though there do seem to be a kind of a swimming in me head at this moment. Maybe that stuff's stronger than it tastes. But I wasn't drunk then, and I'm pretty sure I'm not dotty. I'm haunted, sir, that's what it is – haunted. It might be there was someone killed in one of them houses many years ago, and that's what I see tonight. Perhaps they changed the numbering of the street on account of it – I've heard tell of such things – and when the same night comes round the house goes back to what it was before. But there I am, with a black mark against me, and it ain't a fair trick for no ghost to go getting a plain man into trouble. And I'm sure, sir, you'll agree with me.'

The policeman's narrative had lasted some time, and the hands of the grandfather clock stood at a quarter to five. Peter Wimsey gazed benevolently at his companion, for whom he was beginning to feel a positive affection. He was, if anything, slightly more drunk than the policeman, for he had missed tea and had no appetite for his dinner; but the wine had not clouded his wits; it had only increased excitability and postponed sleep. He said:

'When you looked through the letter-box, could you see any part of the ceiling, or the lights?'

'No, sir; on account, you see, of the flap. I could see right and left and straight forward; but not upwards, and none of the near part of the floor.'

'When you looked at the house from outside, there was no light except through the fanlight. But when you looked through the flap, all the rooms were lit, right and left and at the back?'

'That's so, sir.'

'Are there back doors to the houses?'

'Yes, sir. Coming out of Merriman's End, you turn to the right, and there's an opening a little way along which takes you to the back doors.'

'You seem to have a very distinct visual memory. I wonder if your other kinds of memory are as good. Can you tell me, for instance, whether any of the houses you went into had any particular smell? Especially 10, 12 and 14?'

'Smell, sir?' The policeman closed his eyes to stimulate recollection. 'Why, yes, sir. Number 10, where the two ladies live, that had a sort of an old-fashioned smell. I can't put me tongue to it. Not lavender – but something as ladies keeps in bowls and such – rose-leaves and what not. Pot-pourri, that's the stuff. Pot-pourri. And Number 12 – well, no there was nothing particular there, except I remember thinking they must keep pretty good servants, though we didn't see anybody except the family. All that floor and panelling was polished beautiful – you could see your face in it. Beeswax and turpentine, I says to meself. And elbow-grease. What you'd call a clean house with a good, clean smell. But Number 14 – that was different. I didn't like the smell of that. Stuffy, like as if the nigger had been burning some o' that there incense to his idols, maybe. I never could abide niggers.'

'Ah!' said Peter. 'What you say is very suggestive.' He placed his finger-tips together and shot his last question over them:

'Ever been inside the National Gallery?'

'No, sir,' said the policeman, astonished. 'I can't say as I ever was.'

'That's London again,' said Peter. 'We're the last people in the world to know anything of our great metropolitan institutions. Now, what is the best way to tackle this bunch of toughs, I wonder? It's a little early for a call. Still, there's nothing like doing one's good deed before breakfast, and the sooner you're set right with the sergeant, the better. Let me see. Yes – I think that may do it. Costume pieces are not as a rule in my line, but my routine has been so much upset already, one way and another, that an irregularity more or less will hardly matter. Wait there for me while I have a bath and change. I may be a little time; but it would hardly be decent to get there before six.'

The bath had been an attractive thought, but was perhaps ill-advised, for a curious languor stole over him with the touch of the hot water. The champagne was losing its effervescence. It was with an effort that he dragged himself out and re-awakened himself with a cold shower. The matter of dress required a little thought. A pair of grey flannel trousers was easily found, and though they were rather too well creased for the part he meant to play, he thought that with luck they would probably pass unnoticed. The shirt was a difficulty. His collection of shirts was a notable one, but they were mostly of an inconspicuous and gentlemanly sort. He hesitated for some time over a white shirt with an open sports collar, but decided at length upon a blue one, bought as an experiment and held to be not quite successful. A red tie, if he had possessed such a thing, would have been convincing. After some consideration, he remembered that he had seen his wife in a rather wide Liberty tie, whose prevailing colour was orange. That, he felt, would do if he could find it. On her it had looked rather well; on him, it would be completely abominable. He went through into the next room; it was queer to find it empty. A peculiar sensation came over him. Here *he* was, rifling his wife's drawers, and there *she* was, spirited out of reach at the top of the house with a couple of nurses and an entirely new baby, which might turn into goodness knew what. He sat down before the glass and stared at himself. He felt as though he ought to have changed somehow in the night; but he only looked unshaven and, he thought, a trifle intoxicated. Both were quite good things to look at the moment, though hardly suitable for the father of a family. He pulled out all the drawers in the dressing table; they emitted vaguely familiar smells of face-powder and handkerchief-sachet. He tried the big built-in wardrobe: frocks, costumes and trays full of underwear, which made him feel sentimental. At last he struck a promising vein of gloves and stockings. The next tray held ties, the orange of the desired Liberty creation gleaming in a friendly way among them. He put it on, and observed with pleasure that the effect was Bohemian beyond description. He wandered out again, leaving all the drawers open behind him as though a burglar had passed through the room. An ancient tweed jacket of his own, of a very countrified pattern, suitable only for fishing in Scotland, was next unearthed, together with a pair of brown canvas shoes. He secured his trousers by a belt, searched for and found an old soft-brimmed felt hat of no recognisable colour, and, after removing a few trout-flies from the hat-band and tucking his shirtsleeves well up inside the coat-sleeve, decided that he would do. As an afterthought, he returned to his wife's room and selected a wide woollen scarf in a shade of greenish blue. Thus equipped, he came downstairs again, to find P.C. Burt fast asleep, with his mouth open and snoring.

Peter was hurt. Here he was, sacrificing himself in the interests of this stupid policeman, and the man hadn't the common decency to appreciate it. However, there was no point in waking him yet. He yawned horribly and sat down.

It was the footman who wakened the sleepers at half-past six. If he was surprised to see his master, very strangely attired, slumbering in the hall in company with a large policeman, he was too well-trained to admit the fact even to himself. He merely removed the tray. The faint chink of glass roused Peter, who slept like a cat at all times.

'Hullo, William,' he said. 'Have I overslept myself? What's the time?'

'Five and twenty to seven, my lord.'

'Just about right.' He remembered that the footman slept on the top floor. 'All quiet on the Western Front, William?'

'Not altogether quiet, my lord.' William permitted himself a slight smile. 'The young master was lively about five. But all is satisfactory, I gather from Nurse Jenkyn.'

'Nurse Jenkyn? Is that the young one? Don't let yourself be run away with, William. I say, just give P.C. Burt a light prod in the ribs, would you? He and I have business together.'

In Merriman's End, the activities of the morning were beginning. The milkman came jingling out of the cul-de-sac; lights were twinkling in upper rooms; hands were withdrawing curtains; in front of Number 10, the house maid was already scrubbing the steps. Peter posted his policeman at the top of the street.

'I don't want to make my first appearance with official accompaniment,' he said. 'Come along when I beckon. What by the way is the name of the agreeable gentleman in Number 12? I think he may be of some assistance to us.'

'Mr O'Halloran, sir.'

The policeman looked at Peter expectantly. He seemed to have abandoned all initiative and to place implicit confidence in this hospitable and eccentric gentleman. Peter slouched down the street with his hands in his trousers pocket and his shabby hat pulled rakishly over his eyes. At Number 12 he paused and examined the windows. Those on the ground floor were open; the house was awake. He marched up the steps, took a brief glance through the flap of the letter-box, and rang the bell. A maid in a neat blue dress and white cap and apron opened the door.

'Good morning,' said Peter, slightly raising the shabby hat; 'is Mr O'Halloran in?' He gave the *r* a soft continental roll. 'Not the old gentleman. I mean young Mr O'Halloran?'

'He's in,' said the maid, doubtfully, 'but he isn't up yet.'

'Oh!' said Peter. 'Well it is a little early for a visit. But I desire to see him urgently. I am – there is a little trouble where I live. Could you entreat him – would you be so kind? I have walked all the way,' he added, pathetically, and with perfect truth.

'Have you, sir?' said the maid. She added kindly, 'You do look tired, sir, and that's a fact.'

'It is nothing,' said Peter. 'It is only that I forgot to have any dinner. But if I can see Mr O'Halloran it will be all right.'

'You'd better come in, sir,' said the maid. 'I'll see if I can wake him.' She conducted the exhausted stranger in and offered him a chair. 'What name shall I say, sir?'

'Petrovinsky,' said his lordship, hardily. As he had rather expected, neither the unusual name nor the unusual clothes of this unusually early visitor seemed to cause very much surprise. The maid left him in the tidy little panelled hall and went upstairs without so much as a glance at the umbrella-stand.

Left to himself, Peter sat still, noticing that the hall was remarkably bare of furniture, and was lit by a single electric pendant almost immediately inside the front door. The letter-box was the usual wire cage the bottom of which had been carefully lined with brown paper. From the back of the house came a smell of frying bacon.

Presently there was the sound of somebody running downstairs. A young man appeared in a dressing-gown. He called out as he came: 'Is that you, Stefan? Your name came up as Mr Whisky. Has Marfa run away again, or – What the hell? Who the devil are you, sir?'

'Wimsey,' said Peter, mildly, 'not Whisky; Wimsey the policeman's friend. I just looked in to congratulate you on a mastery of the art of false perspective which I thought had perished with van Hoogstraten, or at least with Grace and Lambelet.'

'Oh!' said the young man. He had a pleasant countenance, with humorous eyes and ears pointed like a faun's. He laughed a little ruefully. 'I suppose my beautiful murder is out. It was too good to last. Those bobbies! I hope to God they gave Number 14 a bad night. May I ask how you come to be involved in the matter?'

'I,' said Peter, 'am the kind of person in whom distressed constables confide – I cannot imagine why. And when I had the picture of that sturdy blue-clad figure, led so persuasively by a Bohemian stranger and invited to peer through a hole, I was irresistibly transported in mind to the National Gallery. Many a time have I squinted sideways through those holes into the little black box, and admired that Dutch interior of many vistas painted so convincingly on the four flat sides of the box. How right you were to preserve your eloquent silence! Your Irish tongue would have given you away. The servants, I gather, were purposely kept out of sight.'

'Tell me,' said Mr O'Halloran, seating himself sideways upon the hall table, 'do you know by heart the occupation of every resident in this quarter of London? I do not paint under my own name.'

'No,' said Peter. 'Like the good Dr Watson, the constable could observe, though he could not reason from his observation; it was the smell of turpentine that betrayed you. I gather that at the time of his first call the apparatus was not very far off.'

'It was folded together and lying under the stairs,' replied the painter. 'It has since been removed to the studio. My father had only just had time to get it out of the way and hitch down the "13" from the fanlight before the police reinforcements arrived.

He had not even time to put back this table I am sitting on; a brief search would have discovered it in the dining room. My father is a remarkable sportsman; I cannot too highly recommend the presence of mind he displayed while I was hareing around the houses and leaving him to hold the fort. It would have been so simple and so unenterprising to explain; but my father, being an Irishman, enjoys treading on the coat-tails of authority.'

'I should like to meet your father. The only thing I do not thoroughly understand is the reason of this elaborate plot. Were you by any chance executing a burglary round the corner, and keeping the police in play while you did it?'

'I never thought of that,' said the young man, with regret in his voice. 'No. The bobby was not the pre-destined victim. He happened to be present at a full-dress rehearsal, and the joke was too good to be lost. The fact is, my uncle is Sir Lucius Preston, the R.A.'

'Ah!' said Peter, 'the light begins to break.'

'My own style of draughtsmanship,' pursued Mr O'Halloran, 'is modern. My uncle has on several occasions informed me that I draw like that only because I do not know how to draw. The idea was that he should be invited to dinner tomorrow and regaled with a story of the mysterious "Number 13", said to appear from time to time in this street and to be haunted by strange noises. Having thus detained him till close upon midnight, I should have set out to see him to the top of the street. As we went along, the cries would have broken out. I should have led him back—'

'Nothing,' said Peter, 'could be more clear. After the preliminary shock, he would have been forced to confess that your draughtsmanship was a triumph of academic accuracy.'

'I hope,' said Mr O'Halloran, 'the performance may still go forward as originally intended.' He looked with some anxiety at Peter, who replied:

'I hope so, indeed. I also hope that your uncle's heart is a strong one. But may I, in the meantime, signal to my unfortunate policeman and relieve his mind? He is in danger of losing his promotion, through a suspicion that he was drunk on duty.'

'Good God!' said Mr O'Halloran. 'No – I don't want that to happen. Fetch him in.'

The difficulty was to make P.C. Burt recognise in the daylight what he had seen by night through the letter-flap. Of the framework of painted canvas, with its forms and figures oddly foreshortened and distorted, he could make little. Only when the thing was set up and lighted in the curtained studio was he at length reluctantly convinced.

'It's wonderful,' he said. 'It's like Maskelyne and Devant. I wish the sergeant could a' seen it.'

'Lure him down here tomorrow night,' said Mr O'Halloran. 'Let him come as my uncle's body-guard. 'You—' he turned to Peter – 'you seem to have a way with policemen. Can't you inveigle the fellow along? Your impersonation of starving and disconsolate Bloomsbury is fully as convincing as mine. How about it?'

'I don't know,' said Peter. 'The costume gives me pain. Besides, is it kind to a p.b. policeman? I give you the R.A., but when it comes to the guardians of the law – Damn it all! I'm a family man, and I must have *some* sense of responsibility.'

Talboys

A LORD PETER WIMSEY STORY

Mr Puffet

'F ather!'
   'Yes, my son.'

'You know those peaches of Mr Puffett's, the whacking great big ones you said I wasn't to take?'

'Well?'

'Well, I've tooken them.'

Lord Peter Wimsey rolled over on his back and stared at his offspring in consternation. His wife laid down her sewing.

'Oh, Bredon, how naughty! Poor Mr Puffett was going to exhibit them at the Flower-Show.'

'Well, Mummy, I didn't mean to. It was a dare.'

Having offered this explanation for what it was

worth, Master Bredon Wimsey again turned candid eyes upon his father, who groaned and sat up.

'And *must* you come and tell me about it? I hope, Bredon, you are not developing into a prig.'

'Well, Father, Mr Puffett saw me. An' he's coming up to have a word with you when he's put on a clean collar.'

'Oh, I see,' said his lordship, relieved. 'And you thought you'd better come and get it over before my temper became further inflamed by hearing his version of the matter?'

'Yes, please, sir.'

'That is rational, at any rate. Very well, Bredon. Go up into my bedroom and prepare for execution. You will find the cane behind the dressing-table.'

'Yes, Father. You won't be long, will you, sir?'

'I shall allow precisely the right time for apprehension and remorse. Off with you!'

The culprit vanished hastily in the direction of the house; the executioner heaved himself to his feet and followed at a leisurely pace, rolling up his sleeves as he went with a certain grimness.

'My dear!' exclaimed Miss Quirk. She gazed in horror through her spectacles at Harriet, who had placidly returned to her patchwork. 'Surely, *surely* you don't allow him to cane that mite of a child.'

'Allow?' said Harriet, amused. 'That's hardly the right word, is it?'

'But Harriet, dear, he oughtn't to do it. You don't realise how dangerous it is. He may ruin the boy's character for life. One must reason with these little people, not break their spirits by brutality. When you inflict pain and humiliation on a child like that, you make him feel helpless and inferior, and all that suppressed resentment will break out later in the most extraordinary and shocking ways.'

'Oh, I don't think he resents it,' said Harriet. 'He's devoted to his father.'

'Well, if he is,' retorted Miss Quirk, 'it must be a sort of masochism, and it ought to be stopped – I mean, it ought to be led gently into some other direction. It's unnatural. How could any one feel a *healthy* devotion for a person who beats him?'

'I can't think; but it often seems to happen. Peter's mother used to lay into him with a slipper, and they've always been the best of friends.'

'If I had a child belonging to me,' said Miss Quirk, 'I would never permit anybody to lay a hand on him. All my little nephews and nieces have been brought up on enlightened modern lines. They never even hear the word, Don't. Now, you see what happens. Just *because* your boy was told *not* to pick the peaches, he picked them. If he hadn't been forbidden to do it, he wouldn't have been disobedient.'

'No,' said Harriet. 'I suppose that's quite true. He

would have picked the peaches just the same, but it wouldn't have been disobedience.'

'Exactly,' cried Miss Quirk, triumphantly. 'You see – you manufacture a crime and then punish the poor child for it. Besides, if it hadn't been for the prohibition, he'd have left the fruit alone.'

'You don't know Bredon. He never leaves anything alone.'

'Of course not,' said Miss Quirk, 'and, he never will, so long as you surround him with prohibitions. His meddling with what doesn't belong to him is just an act of defiance.'

'He's not defiant very often,' said Harriet, 'but of course it's very difficult to refuse a dare from a big boy like George Waggett. I expect it was George; it usually is.'

'No doubt,' observed Miss Quirk, 'the village children are all brought up in an atmosphere of faultfinding and defiance. That kind of thing is contagious. Democratic principles are all very well, but I should scarcely have thought it wise to expose your little boy to contamination.'

'Would you forbid him to play with George Waggett?'

'I should never *forbid* anything. I should endeavour to suggest some more suitable companion. Bredon could be encouraged to look after his little brother; that would give him a useful outlet for his energies and allow him to feel himself important.'

'Oh, but he's really very good with Roger,' said Harriet, equably. She looked up, to see chastiser and chastised emerging from the house, hand in hand. 'They seem to be quite good friends. Bredon was rather uplifted when he was promoted to a cane; he thinks it dignified and grown-up . . . . Well, ruffian, how many did you get?'

'Three,' said Master Bredon, confidentially. 'Awful hard ones. One for being naughty, an' one for being young ass enough to be caught, and one for making a 'fernal nuisance of myself on a hot day.'

'Oh, dear,' said Miss Quick, appalled by the immorality of all this. 'And are you sorry for having taken poor Mr. Puffett's peaches, so that he can't get a prize at the Show.'

Bredon looked at her in astonishment.

'We've done all that,' he said, with a touch of indignation. His father thought it well to intervene.

'It's a rule in this household,' he announced, 'that once we've been whacked, nothing more can be said. The topic is withdrawn from circulation.'

'Oh,' said Miss Quirk. She still felt that something ought to be done to compensate the victim of brutality and relieve his repressions. 'Well, as you're a good boy, would you like to come and sit on my knee?'

'No thank you,' said Bredon. Training, or natural politeness, prompted him to amplify the refusal. 'Thank you very much all the same.'

'A more tactless suggestion,' said Peter, 'I never heard.' He dropped into a deck-chair, picked up his son and heir by the waist-belt and slung him face downwards across his knees. 'You'll have to eat your tea on all-fours, like Nebuchadnezzar.'

'Who was Nebuchadnezzar?'

'Nebuchadnezzar, the King of the Jews—' began Peter. His version of that monarch's inquities was interrupted by the appearance, from behind the house, of a stout figure, unsuitably clad for the season in sweater, corduroy trousers and bowler hat. 'The curse is come upon me, cried the Lady of Shalott.'

'Who was the Lady of Shalott?'

'I'll tell you at bedtime. Here is Mr. Puffett, breathing out threatenings and slaughter. We must now stand up and face the music. 'Afternoon, Puffett.'

'Arternoon, me lord and me lady,' said Mr Puffett. He removed his bowler and mopped his streaming brow. 'And miss,' he added, with a vague gesture in Miss Quirk's direction. 'I made bold, me lord, to come round—'

'That,' said Peter, 'was very kind of you. Otherwise, of course, we should have come to see you and say we were sorry. We were overcome by a sudden irresistible impulse, attributable, we think, to the beauty of the fruit and the exciting nature of the enterprise. We hope very much that we have left enough for the Flower-Show, and we will be careful not to do it again. We should like to mention that a measure of justice has already been done, in the shape of three of the juiciest, but if there is anything further coming to us, we shall try to receive it in a becoming spirit of penitence.'

'Well, there!' said Mr Puffett. 'If I didn't say to Jinny, "Jinny," I says, "I 'ope the young gentleman doesn't tell 'is lordship. He'll be main angry," I says, "and I wouldn't wonder if 'e didn't wallop 'im." "Oh Dad," she says, "run up quick, never mind your Sunday coat, and tell 'is lordship as 'e didn't take only two peaches and there's plenty left," she says. So I comes as quick as I can, only I 'ad ter wash, what with doin' out the pigstyes, and jest to put on a clean collar; but not bein' as young as I was, and gettin' stout-like, I don't get up the 'ill as quick as I might. There wasn't no call to thrash the young gentleman, me lord, me 'avin' caught 'im afore much 'arm was done. Boys will be boys – and I'll lay what you like it was some of them other young devils put 'im up to it, begging your pardon, me lady.'

'Well, Bredon,' said his father; 'it's very kind of

Mr Puffett to take that view of it. Suppose you go with him up to the house and ask Bunter to draw him a glass of beer. And on the way, you may say whatever your good feeling may suggest.'

He waited till the oddly-assorted couple were half-way across the lawn, and then called 'Puffett?'

'Me lord?' said Mr Puffett, returning alone.

'Was there really much damage done?'

'No, me lord. Only two peaches, like I said. I jest popped out from be'ind the potting-shed in time, and 'e was off like one o'clock.'

'Thank heaven! From what he said, I was afraid he had wolfed the lot. And, look here, Puffett. Don't ask him who put him up to it. I shouldn't imagine he'd tell, but he might fancy he was a bit of a hero for refusing.'

'I get you,' said Mr Puffett. ''E's a proper 'igh-sperrited young gentleman, ain't 'e?' He winked, and went ponderously to rejoin his penitent robber.

The episode was considered closed; and everybody (except Miss Quirk) was surprised when Mr Puffett arrived next morning at breakfast-time and announced without preliminary:

'Beg pardon, me lord, but all my peaches 'as bin took in the night, and I'd be glad to know 'oo done it.'

'All your peaches taken, Puffett?'

'Every blessed one on 'em, me lord, practically speakin.' And the Flower-Show ter-morrer.'

'Coo!' said Master Bredon. He looked up from his plate, and found Miss Quirk's eye fixed upon him.

'That's a dirty trick,' said his lordship. 'Have you any idea who it was? Or would you like me to come and look into the matter for you?'

Mr Puffett turned his bowler hat slowly over between his large hands.

'Not wishin' yer lordship ter put yerself out,' he said slowly. 'But it jest crossed me mind as summun at the 'ouse might be able ter throw light, as it were, upon the subjick.'

'I shouldn't think so,' said Peter, 'but it's easy to ask. Harriet, do you by any chance know anything about the disappearance of Puffett's peaches?'

Harriet shook her head.

'Not a thing. Roger, dear, please eat your egg not quite so splashily. You've given yourself a moustache like Mr Billing's.'

'Can you give us any help, Bredon?'

'No.'

'No, what?'

'No, sir. Please, Mummy, may I get down?'

'Just a minute, darling. You haven't folded up your napkin.'

'Oh, sorry.'

'Miss Quirk?'

Miss Quirk was so much aghast at hearing this flat denial, that she had remained staring at the eldest Master Wimsey, and started on hearing herself addressed.

'Do *I* know anything? Well!' She hesitated. 'Now, Bredon, am I to tell Daddy? Wouldn't you rather do it yourself?' Bredon shot a quick look at his father, but made no answer. That was only to be expected. Beat a child, and you make him a liar and a coward. 'Come now,' said Miss Quirk, coaxingly, 'it would be *ever* so much nicer and better and braver to own up, don't you think? It'll make Mummy and Daddy very very sad if you leave it to *me* to tell them.'

'To tell us what?' inquired Harriet.

'My dear Harriet,' said Miss Quirk, annoyed by this foolish question, 'if I tell you *what*, then I've told you, haven't I? And I'm quite *sure* Bredon would much rather tell you himself.'

'Bredon,' said his father, 'have you any idea what Miss Quirk thinks you ought to tell us? Because, if so, you could tell us and we could get on.'

'No, sir. I don't know anything about Mr Puffett's peaches. May I get down *now*, Mummy, please?'

'Oh, Bredon!' cried Miss Quirk, reproachfully. 'When I saw you, you know, with my own eyes!

Ever so early – at five o'clock this morning. Now, won't you say what you were doing?'

'Oh, that!' said Bredon; and blushed. Mr Puffett scratched his head.

'What were you doing?' asked Harriet, gently. 'Not anything naughty, darling, were you? Or is it a secret?'

Bredon nodded. 'Yes, it's a secret. Something we were doing.' He sighed. 'I don't think it's naughty, Mum.'

'I expect it is though,' said Peter in a resigned tone. 'Your secrets so often are. Quite unintentionally, no doubt, but they do have a tendency that way. Be warned in time, Bredon, and undo it, or stop doing it, before I discover it. I understand it had nothing to do with Mr Puffett's peaches?'

'Oh, no, Father. Please, Mummy, may I—'

'Yes, dear, you may get down. But you must ask Miss Quirk to excuse you.'

'Please, Miss Quirk, will you excuse me?'

'Yes, certainly,' said Miss Quirk in a mournful tone. Bredon scrambled down hastily, said, 'I'm *very* sorry about your peaches, Mr Puffett,' and made his escape.

'I am sorry to have to say it,' said Miss Quirk, 'but I think, Mr Puffett, you will find your peaches in the woodshed. I woke up early this morning, and I saw Bredon and another little boy crossing the

121

yard, carrying something between them in a bucket. I waved at them from the window, and they hurried off to the woodshed in what I *can* only call a furtive kind of way.'

'Well, Puffett,' said his lordship, 'I'm sorry about this. Shall I come up and take a look at the place? Or do you wish to search the woodshed? I am quite sure you will not find your peaches there, though I should hesitate to say what else you might not find.'

'I'd be grateful,' replied Mr Puffett, 'to 'ave yer advice, me lord, if so be as you could spare the time. What beats me, it's a wide bed, and yet there ain't no footprints, in a manner of speaking, except as it might be young master's, there. Which, footprints bein' in a manner your lordship's walk in life, I made bold to come. But, Master Bredon 'avin' said it weren't him, I reckon them marks 'll be wot'e left yesterday, though 'ow a man or a boy either could cross that there bed of damp earth and not leave no sign of 'imself, unless 'e wos a bird, is more than I can make out, nor Jinny neither.'

Mr Tom Puffett was proud of his walled garden. He had built the wall himself (for he was a builder by trade), and it was a handsome brick structure, ten feet high, and topped on all four sides with a noble parapet of broken bottle-glass. The garden lay on the opposite side of the road from the little house

122

where its owner lived with his daughter and son-in-law, and possessed a solid wooden gate, locked at night with a padlock. On either side of it were flourishing orchards; at the back ran a deeply rutted lane, still muddy – for the summer, up to the last few days, had been a wet one.

'That there gate,' said Mr Puffett, 'was locked last night at nine o'clock as ever is, 'an it was still locked when I came in at seven this mornin'; so 'ooever done it 'ad to climb this yer wall.'

'So I see,' replied Lord Peter. 'My demon child is of tender years; still, I admit that he is capable of almost anything, when suitably inspired and assisted. But I don't think he would have done it after yesterday's little incident, and I am positive that if he had done it, he'd have said so.'

'Reckon you're right,' agreed Mr Puffett, unlocking the door, 'though when I was a nipper like 'im, if I'd 'ad that old woman a-joring' at me, I'd a' said anythink.'

'So'd I,' said Peter. 'She's a friend of my sister-in-law's, said to need a country holiday. I feel we shall all shortly need a town holiday. Your plums seem to be doing well. H'm. A pebble path isn't the best medium for showing footprints.'

'That it's not,' admitted Mr Puffett. He led the way between the neat flower and vegetable beds to the far end of the garden. Here at the foot of the wall was a border about nine feet wide, the middle section of which was empty except for some rows of late-sown peas. At the back, trained against the wall, stood the peach-tree, on which one great, solitary fruit glowed rosily among the dark leafage. Across the bed ran a double line of small footprints.

'Did you hoe this bed over after my son's visit yesterday?'

'No, my lord.'

'Then he hasn't been here since. Those are his marks all right – I ought to know; I see enough of them on my own flower-beds.' Peter's mouth twitched a little. 'Look! He came very softly, trying most honorably not to tread on the peas. He pinched a peach and bolted it where he stood. I enquire, with a parent's natural anxiety, whether he ejected the stone, and observe, with relief, that he did. He moved on, he took a second peach, you popped out from the potting-shed, he started like a guilty thing and ran off in a hurry – this time, I am sorry to see, trampling on the peas. I hope he deposited the second peach-stone somewhere. Well, Puffett, you're right; there are no other footprints. Could the thief have put down a plank and walked on that, I wonder?'

'There's no planks here,' said Mr Puffett, 'except the little 'un I uses meself for bedding-out. That's three feet long or thereabouts. Would yer like ter look at it, me lord?'

'No good. A little reflection shows that one cannot cross a nine-foot bed on a three-foot plank without shifting the plank, and that one cannot at the same time stand on the plank and shift it. You're sure there's only one? Yes? Then that's washed out.'

'Could 'e a'brought one with 'im?'

'The orchard walls are high and hard to climb, even without the additional encumbrance of a nine-foot plank. Besides, I'm almost sure no plank has been used. I think, if it had, the edges would have left some mark. No, Puffett, nobody crossed this bed. By the way, doesn't it strike you as odd that the thief should have left just one big peach behind? It's pretty conspicuous. Was that done merely to point the joke? Or – wait a minute, what's that?'

Something had caught his eye at the back of the box border, some dozen feet to the right of where they were standing. He picked it up. It was a peach; firm and red and not quite ripe. He stood weighing it thoughtfully in his hand.

'Having picked the peach, he found it wasn't ripe and chucked it away in a temper. Is that likely, Puffett, do you think? And unless I am mistaken, there are quite a number of green leaves scattered about the foot of the tree. How often, when one picks a peach, does one break off the leaves as well?'

He looked expectantly at Mr Puffett, who returned no answer.

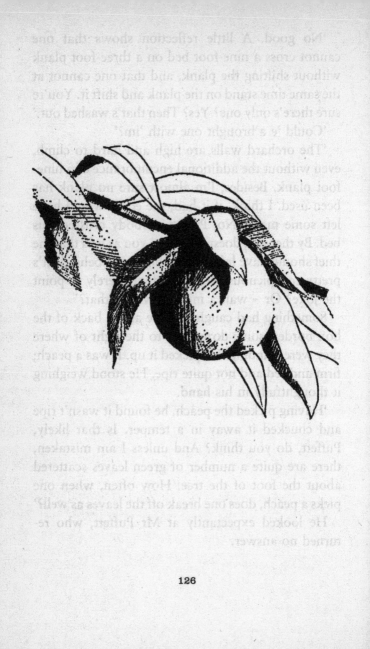

'I think,' went on Peter, 'we will go and have a look in the lane.'

Immediately behind the wall ran a rough grass verge. Mr Puffett, leading the way to this, was peremptorily waved back, and was thereafter treated to a fine exposition of detective work in the traditional manner; his lordship, extended on his stomach, thrusting his long nose and long fingers delicately through each successive tuft of grass, Mr Puffett himself, stooping with legs well apart and hands on knees, peering anxiously at him from the edge of the lane. Presently the sleuth sat up on his heels and said:

'Here you are, Puffett. There were two men. They came up the lane from the direction of the village, wearing hob-nailed boots and carrying a ladder between them. They set up the ladder *here*; the grass, you see, is still a little bent, and there are two deepish dents in the soil. One man climbed to the top and took the peaches, while the other, I think, stood at the foot to keep guard and receive the fruit in a bag or basket or something. This isn't a case of larking youngsters, Puffett; from the length of the strides they were grown men. What enemies have you made in your harmless career? Or who are your chief rivals in the peach class?'

'Well, there,' said Mr Puffett, slowly. 'There's the Vicar shows peaches, and Dr Jellyband from Great

Pagford, and Jack Baker – he's the policeman, you know, came when Joe Sellon went off to Canada. And there's old Critch; him and me had a dispute about a chimbley. And Maggs the blacksmith – 'e didn't 'arf like it w'en I wiped 'is eye last year with me vegetable marrers. Oh, and Waggett the butcher, 'e shows peaches. But I dunno as any o' them 'ud do me a turn like this 'ere. But 'ere, me lord, 'ow did they *get* the peaches? They couldn't reach 'em from the top of the ladder, nor yet off the wall, let alone sitting on them there bottles. The top o' the tree's five foot below the top o' the wall.'

'That's simple,' said Peter. 'Think of the broken leaves and the peach in the box border, and consider how *you* would have done it. By the way, if you want proof that the robbing was done from this side, get a ladder and look over. I'll lay you anything you like, you'll find that the one peach that was left is hidden by the leaves from anybody looking *down* on it, though it's clearly enough seen from the garden. No, there's no difficulty about how it was done; the difficulty is to put one's hand on the culprits. Unfortunately, there's no footprints clear enough to show the complete pattern of the hob-nails.'

He considered a moment, while Mr Puffett watched him with the air of one confidently expecting a good conjuring trick.

'One could make a house-to-house visitation,' went on his lordship, 'and ask questions, or search. But it's surprising how things disappear, and how people dry up when asked direct questions. Children especially. Look here, Puffett, I'm not at all sure my prodigal son mightn't be able to throw some light on this, after all. But leave me to conduct the examination, it may need delicate handling.'

There is one drawback about retreating to a really small place in the country and leaving behind you the stately publicity of town life in a house with ten servants. When you have tucked in yourselves, and your three children, and your indispensable man and your one equally indispensable and devoted maid, both time and space become rather fully occupied. You may, by taking your husband into your own room and accommodating the two elder boys in his dressing-room, squeeze in an extra person who, like Miss Quirk, has been wished upon you; but it is scarcely possible to run after her all day to see that she is not getting into mischief. This is more particularly the case if you are a novelist by profession, and if moreover, your idea of a happy holiday is to dispose as completely and briskly as possible of children, book, servants and visitor, so as to snatch all the available moments for playing the fool with a congenial, but admittedly distracting, husband. Harriet Wimsey, writing for dear life in the sitting-room, kept one eye on her paper and the other on Master Paul Wimsey, who was disembowelling his old stuffed rabbit in the window-seat. Her ears were open for a yell from young Roger, whose rough-and-tumble with the puppy on the lawn might at any moment end in disaster. Her consciousness was occupied with her plot, her subconsciousness with the fact that she was three months behind on her contract. If she gave an occasional vague thought to her first-born, it was only to wonder whether he was hindering Bunter at his work, or merely concocting, in his own quiet way, some more than usually hideous shock for his parents. Himself was the last person he ever damaged; he was a child with a singular talent for falling on his feet. She had no attention to spare for Miss Quirk.

Miss Quirk had tried the woodshed, but it was empty, and among its contents she could find nothing more suspicious than a hatchet, a saw, a rabbit-hutch, a piece of old carpet and a wet ring among the sawdust. She was not surprised that the evidence had been removed; Bredon had been extraordinarily anxious to leave the breakfast-table, and his parents had shut their eyes and let him go. Nor had Peter troubled to examine the premises; he had walked straight out of the house with that man Puffett, who naturally could not insist upon a search. Both Peter and Harriet were obviously burking inquiry; they did not want to admit the consequences of their wickedly mistaken system of training.

'Mummy! come out an' play wiv' me an' Bom-bom!'

'Presently, darling. I've only got a little bit to finish.'

'When's presently, Mummy?'

'Very soon. In about ten minutes.'

'What's ten minutes, Mummy?'

Harriet laid down her pen. As a conscientious parent, she could not let this opportunity pass. Four years old was said to be too early, but children differed and you never knew.

'Look, darling. Here's the clock. When this long hand gets to *that*, that'll be ten minutes.'

'When *this* gets to *that*?'

'Yes, darling. Sit quiet just for a little bit and look after it and tell me when it gets there.'

An interval. Miss Quirk had by this time searched the garage, the greenhouse and the shed that housed the electric plant.

'It isn't moving, Mummy.'

'Yes, it is, really, only it goes very, *very* slowly. You'll have to keep a very sharp eye on it.'

Miss Quirk had reached the back parts of the house itself. She entered by the back door, and passed through the scullery into a passage, containing, among other things, the door of the boot-hole. In this retreat, she discovered a small village maiden, cleaning a pair of very youthful boots.

'Have you seen –?' began Miss Quirk. Then her eye fell on the boots. 'Are those Master Bredon's boots?'

'Yes, miss,' said the girl, with the startled look peculiar to young servants when suddenly questioned by strangers.

'They're very dirty,' said Miss Quirk. She remembered that Bredon had worn clean sandals when he came in to breakfast. 'Give those to me for a moment,' said Miss Quirk.

The small maid looked round with a gasp for advice and assistance, but both Bunter and the maid seemed to be occupied elsewhere, and one could not refuse a request from a lady staying in the house. Miss Quirk took charge of the boots. 'I'll bring them back presently,' she said, with a nod, and passed on. Fresh, damp earth on Bredon's boots, and something secret brought home in a pail – it scarcely needed a Peter Wimsey to put two and two together. But Peter Wimsey was refusing to detect in the right place. Miss Quirk would show him.

Miss Quirk went on along the passage and came

to a door. As she approached it, it opened and Bredon's face, very dirty, appeared round the edge. At sight of her, it popped in again like a bolting rabbit.

'Ah!' said Miss Quirk. She pushed the door briskly. But even a child of six, if he can reach it and is determined, can make proper use of a bolt.

'Roger, darling, no! Shaking won't make it go any faster. It'll only give the poor clock tummyache. Oh, look, what a dreadful mess Paul's made with his rabbit. Help him pick up the bits, dear, and then you'll see, the ten minutes will be up.'

Peter, returning from Mr Puffett's garden, found his wife and two-thirds of his family rolling vigorously about the lawn with Bom-bom. Being invited to roll, he rolled, but with only half his attention.

'It's a curious thing,' he observed plaintively, 'that though my family makes a great deal of noise and always seems to be on top of me' (this was, at the moment, a fact), 'I never can lay hands on the bit of it I want at the moment. Where is the pest, Bredon?'

'I haven't dared to ask.'

Peter rose up, with his youngest son clinging, leech-like, to his shoulder, and went in search of Bunter, who knew everything without asking.

'Master Bredon, my lord, is engaged at present in

an altercation with Miss Quirk through the furnace-room door.'

'Good God, Bunter! Which of them is inside?'

'Master Bredon, my lord.'

'I breathe again. I feared we might have to effect a rescue. Catch hold of this incubus, will you, and hand him back to her ladyship.'

All Miss Quirk's coaxing had been impotent to lure Bredon out of the furnace-room. At Peter's voice she turned quickly.

'Oh, Peter! Do get the child to come out. He's got those peaches in there, and I'm sure he'll make himself ill.'

Lord Peter raised his already sufficiently surprised eyebrows.

'If your expert efforts fail,' said he, 'will my brutal threats have any effect, do you suppose? Besides, even if he *were* eating peaches, ought we, in this peremptory way, to suppress that natural expression of his personality? And whatever makes you imagine that we keep peaches in the furnace-room?'

'I know he's got them there,' said Miss Quirk. 'And I don't blame the child. If you beat a boy for stealing, he'll steal again. Besides, look at these boots he went out in this morning – all covered with damp mould.'

Lord Peter took the boots and examined them with interest.

'Elementary, my dear Watson. But allow me to suggest that some training is necessary, even for the work of a practical domestic detective. This mould is not the same colour as the mould in Puffett's garden, and in fact is not garden mould at all. Further, if you take the trouble to look at the flower-beds, you will see that they are not wet enough to leave as much mud as this on a pair of boots. Thirdly, I can do all the detective work required in this family. And fourthly, you might realise that it is rather discourteous of you to insist that my son is a liar.'

'Very well,' said Miss Quirk, a little red in the face. 'Fetch him out of there, and you'll see.'

'But why should I fetch him out, and implant a horrible frustration-complex around the furnace-room?'

'As you like,' said Miss Quirk. 'It's no business of mine.'

'True,' said Peter. He watched her stride angrily away, and said:

'Bredon! You can come out. She's gone.'

There was a sound of the sliding of iron, and his son slithered out like an eel, pulling the door carefully to behind him.

'You're not very clean, are you?' said his father, dispassionately. 'It looks to me as though the furnace-room needed dusting. I'm not very clean myself, if it comes to that. I've been crawling in the lane behind Mr Puffett's garden, trying to find out who stole his peaches.'

'*She* says *I* did.'

'I'll tell you a secret, Bredon. Grown-up people don't always know everything, though they try to pretend they do. That is called "prestige" and is responsible for most of the wars that devastate the continent of Europe.'

'I think,' said Bredon, who was accustomed to his father's meaningless outbursts of speech, 'she's silly.'

'So do I; but don't say I said so.'

'And rude.'

'*And* rude. I, on the other hand, am silly, but seldom rude. Your mother is neither rude nor silly.'

'Which am I?'

'You are an egotistical extravert of the most irrepressible type. Why do you wear boots when you go mud-larking? It's much less trouble to clean your feet than your boots.'

'There's thistles and nettles.'

'True, O King! Yes, I know the place now. Down by the stream, at the far end of the paddock. . . . Is that the Secret you've got in the furnace-room?'

Bredon nodded, his mouth obstinately shut.

'Can't you let me in on it?'

Bredon shook his head.

136

'No, I don't think so,' he explained candidly. 'You see, you might feel you ought to stop it.'

'That's awkward. It's so often my duty to stop things. Miss Quirk thinks I oughtn't ever to stop anything, but I don't feel I can go quite as far as that. I wonder what the devil you've been up to. We've had newts and frogs and sticklebacks, and tadpoles are out of season. I hope it isn't adders, Bredon, or you'll swell up and turn purple. I can stand for most livestock, but not adders.'

'Tisn' *tadders*,' replied his son, with dawning hope. 'Only very nearly. An' I don't know what it lives on. I say, if you will let me keep it, d'you mind coming in quick, 'cos I 'spect it's creeped out of the bucket.'

'In that case,' said his lordship, 'I think we'd better conduct a search of the premises instantly. My nerves are fairly good; but if it were to go up the flue and come out in the kitchen—'

He followed his offspring hastily into the furnace-room.

'I wish,' said Harriet, a little irritably, for she strongly disliked being lectured about her duties and being thus prevented from attending to them, 'you wouldn't always talk about "a" child, as if all children were alike. Even my three are all quite different.'

'Mothers always think their own children are different,' said Miss Quirk. 'But the fundamental principles of child-psychology are the same in all, I have studied the subject. Take this question of punishment. When you punish a child—'

'*Which* child?'

'Any child – you harm the delicate mechanism of its reaction to life. Some become hardened, some become cowed, but in either case you set up a feeling of inferiority.'

'It's not so simple. Don't take any child – take mine. If you reason with Bredon, he gets obstinate. He knows perfectly well when he's been naughty, and sometimes he prefers to be naughty and take the consequences. Roger's another matter. I don't think we shall ever whip Roger, because he's sensitive and easily frightened and rather likes having his feelings appealed to. But he's already beginning to feel a little inferior to Bredon, because he isn't allowed to be whipped. I suppose we shall have to persuade him that whipping is part of the eldest son's pre-rogative. Which will be all right provided we don't have to whip Paul.'

There were so many dreadful errors in this speech, that Miss Quirk scarcely knew where to begin.

'I think it's such a mistake to let the younger ones fancy that there is anything superior in being the eldest. My little nephews and nieces—'

'Yes,' said Harriet. 'But one's got to prepare people for life, hasn't one? The day is bound to come when they realise that all Peter's real property is entailed.'

Miss Quirk said she so much preferred the French custom of dividing all property equally. 'It's *so* much better for the children.'

'Yes; but it's very bad for the property.'

'But Peter wouldn't put his property before his children!'

Harriet smiled.

'My dear Miss Quirk! Peter's fifty-two, and he's reverting to type.'

Peter at that moment was not looking or behaving like fifty-two, but he was rapidly reverting to a much more ancient and early type than the English landed gentleman. He had, with some difficulty, retrieved the serpent from the ash-hole, and now sat on a heap of clinker, watching it as it squirmed at the bottom of the bucket.

'Golly, what a whopper!' he said, reverently. 'How did you catch him, old man?'

'Well, we went to get minnows, and he came swimming along, and Joey Maggs caught him in his net. And he wanted to kill him along of biting, but I said he couldn't bite, 'cos you told us the difference between snakes. And Joe bet me I

139

wouldn't let him bite me, an' I said I didn' mind and he said, is it a dare? an' I said, Yes, if I can have him afterwards, so I let him bite me, only of course he didn' bite an' George helped me bring him back in the bucket.'

'So Joey Maggs caught him in his net, did he?'

'Yes, but *I* knew he wasn't a nadder. And please, sir, will you give me a net, 'cos Joe's got a lovely big one, only he was awfully late this morning and we thought he wasn't coming, and he said somebody had hidden his net.'

'Did he? That's very interesting.'

'Yes. May I have a net, please?'

'You may.'

'Oh, thank-you, Father. May I keep him, please, and what does he live on?'

'Beetles, I think.' Peter plunged his hand into the bucket, and the snake wound itself about his wrist and slithered along his arm. 'Come on, Cuthbert. You remind me of when I was at my prep. school, and we put one the dead spit of you into—' He caught himself up, too late.

'Where, Father?'

'Well, there was a master we all hated, and we put a snake in his bed. It's rather frequently done. In fact, I believe it's what grass-snakes are for.'

'Is it very naughty to put snakes in people you don't like's beds?'

140

'Yes. Exceedingly naughty. No nice boy would ever think of doing such a thing. . . . I say, *Bredon*—'

Harriet Wimsey sometimes found her eldest son disconcerting. 'You know, Peter, he's a most un-convincing-looking child. *I* know he's yours, be-cause there is nobody else's he could be. And the colour's more or less right. But where on earth did he get that square, stolid appearance, and that incredible snub nose?'

But at that instant, in the furnace-room, over the body of the writhing Cuthbert, square-face and hatchet-face stared at one another and grew into an awful, impish likeness.

'Oh, Father!'

'I don't know what your mother will say. We shall get into most frightful trouble. You'd better leave it to me. Cut along now, and ask Bunter if he's got such a thing as a strong flour-bag and a stout piece of string, because you'll never make Cuthbert stay in this bucket. And for God's sake, don't go about looking like Guy Fawkes and Gunpowder Treason. When you've brought the bag, go and wash yourself. I want you to run down with a note to Mr Puffett.'

Mr Puffett made his final appearance just after dinner, explaining that he had not been able to come earlier, 'along of a job out Lopsley way.' He was both grateful and astonished.

'To think of it being old Billy Maggs and that brother of his, and all along o' them perishin 'old vegetable marrers. You wouldn't think a chap cud 'arbour a grievance that way, would yer? 'Tain't even as though 'e wor a'showin' peaches of his own. It beat me. Said'e did it for a joke. "Joke?" I says to 'im. "I'd like to 'ear wot the magistrate ud say to that there kinder joke." Owsumdever, I got me peaches back, and the Show being ter-morrer, mebbe they won't 'ave took no 'arm. Good thing 'im and they boys 'adn't 'ave ate the lot.'

The household congratulated Mr Puffett on this happy termination to the incident, Mr Puffett chuckled.

'Ter think o' Billy Maggs an' that good-fer-nothin' brother of 'is a-standin' on that there ladder a-fishin' for any peaches with young Joey's stickle-back net. A proper silly sight they'd a-bin if any-body'd come that way. "Think yerselves clever," I says to Bill. "W'y, 'is lordship didn't only cast one eye over the place afore 'e says, 'W'y, Puffett,' e' says, ' 'ere's Billy Maggs an' that there brother of 'is been a-wallerin' all over your wall like a 'erd of elephants.' " Ah! An' a proper fool 'e looked. 'Course, I see now it couldn't only a'been a net, knockin' the leaves about that way. But that there unripe 'un got away from 'im all right "Bill," I says, "you'll never make no fisherman, lettin' 'em get away from you like that." Pulled 'is leg proper, I did. But see 'ere, me lord, 'ow did you come ter know it was Billy Maggs's Joey's net? 'E ain't the only one.'

'A little judicious inquiry in the proper quarter,' replied his lordship. 'Billy Maggs's Joe gave the show away, unbeknownst. But see here, Puffett, don't blame Joe. He knew nothing about it, nor did my boy. Only from something Joe said to Bredon I put two and two together.'

'Ah!' said Mr Puffett, 'an' that reminds me. I've got more peaches back nor I wants for the Show, so I made bold to bring 'arf-a-dozen round for Master Bredon. I don't mind tellin' you, I did think for about 'arf a minute it might a' bin 'im. Only 'arf a minute, mind you – but knowin' wot boys is, I did jest think it might be.'

'It's very kind of you,' said Harriet. 'Bredon's in bed now, but we'll give them to him in the morning. He'll enjoy them so much and be so pleased to know you've quite forgiven him for those other two.'

'Oh, *them*!' replied Mr Puffett. 'Don't you say nothing more about them. Jest a bit o' fun, that wos. Well, goodnight all, and many thanks to your lordship. Coo!' said Mr Puffett, as Peter escorted him to the door, 'ter think o' Billy Maggs and that there spindle-shanked brother of 'is a-fishin' for peaches with a kid's net a-top o' my wall. I didden 'arf make 'em all laugh round at the Crown.'

Miss Quirk had said nothing, Peter slipped upstairs by the back way, through Harriet's bedroom into his own. In the big four-poster, one boy was asleep, but the other sat up at his cautious approach.

'Have you done the deed, Mr Scatterblood?'

'No, Cap'n Teach, but your orders shall be carried out in one twirl of a marlin spike. In the meantime, the bold Mr Puffett has recovered his lost treasure and has haled the criminals up before him and had them hanged at the yardarm after a drum-head court-martial. He has sent you a share of the loot.'

'Oh, good egg! what did *she* say?'

'Nothing. Mind you, Bredon, if she apologises, we'll have to call Cuthbert off. A guest is a guest, so long as she behaves like a gentleman.'

'Yes, I see. Oh, I do hope she won't apologise!'

'That's a very immoral thing to hope. If you bounce like that, you'll wake your brother.'

'Father! Do you think she'll fall down in a fit an' foam at the mouth?'

'I sincerely hope not. As it is, I'm taking my life in my hands. If I perish in the attempt, remember I was true to the Jolly Roger. Good night, Cap'n Teach.'

'Good-night, Mr Scatterblood. I *do* love you.'

Lord Peter Wimsey embraced his son, assumed the personality of Mr Scatterblood and crept softly down the back way to the furnace-room. Cuthbert, safe in his bag, was drowsing upon a hot-water bottle, and made no demonstration as he was borne upstairs.

Miss Quirk did not apologise, and the subject of peaches was not mentioned again. But she may have sensed a certain constraint in the atmosphere, for she rose rather earlier than usual, saying she was tired and thought she would go to bed.

'Peter,' said Harriet, when they were alone: 'what *are* you and Bredon up to? You have both been so unnaturally quiet since lunch. You must be in some sort of mischief.'

'To a Teach or a Scatterblood,' said Peter with dignity, 'There is no such word as mischief. We call it piracy on the high seas.'

'I knew it,' replied Harriet, resignedly. 'If I'd realised the disastrous effect sons would have on your character, I'd never have trusted you with any. Oh, dear! I'm thankful that woman's gone to bed; she's *so* in the way.'

'Isn't she? I think she must have picked up her infant psychology from the Woman's page in the *Morning Mercury*. Harriet, absolve me now from all my sins of the future, so that I may enjoy them without remorse.'

His wife was not unmoved by this appeal, only observing after an interval, 'There's something deplorably frivolous about making love to one's wife after seven years of marriage. Is it my lord's pleasure to come to bed?'

'It is your lord's very great pleasure.'

My lord, who in the uncanonical process of obtaining absolution without confession or penitence, had almost lost sight of the sin, was recalled to himself by his wife's exclamation as they passed through the outer bedroom:

'Peter! Where is Bredon?'

He was saved from having to reply by a succession of long and blood-curdling shrieks, followed by a confused outcry.

'Heavens!' said Harriet. 'Something's happened to Paul!' She shot through her own room on to the Privy Stair, which, by a subsidiary flight, communicated with the back bedrooms. Peter followed more slowly.

On the landing stood Miss Quirk in her nightgown. She had Bredon's head tucked under her arm, and was smacking him with impressive though ill-directed energy. She continued to shriek as she smacked. Bredon, accustomed to a more scientific discipline, was taking the situation stolidly, but the nursemaid, with her head thrust out of an adjacent door, was crying, 'Lor', whatever is it?' Bunter, clattering down from the attic in his pyjamas with a long pair of firetongs in his hand, pulled up short in observing his master and mistress, and, with some dim recollection of his military service, brought his weapon to the present.

Peter seized Miss Quirk by the arm and extricated his son's head from chancery.

'Dear me!' he said. 'I thought you objected to corporal chastisement.'

Miss Quirk was in no mood for ethical discussion.

'That horrible boy!' she said, panting. 'He put a snake in my bed. A disgusting, slimy snake. A snake!'

'Another erroneous inference,' said Peter. 'I put it there myself.'

'You? *You* put a snake in my bed?'

'But I knew all about it,' put in Bredon, anxious that the honour and blame should be equitably distributed. 'It was all his idea, but it was my snake.'

His father rounded upon him. 'I didn't tell *you* to come wandering out of your bed.'

'No, sir: but you didn't tell me not to.'

'Well,' said Peter, with a certain grimness, 'you got what you came for.' He rubbed his son's rump in a comforting manner.

'Huh!' said Bredon. '*She* can't whack for toffee.'

'May I ask,' demanded Miss Quirk with trembling dignity, '*why* I should have been subjected to this abominable outrage?'

'I fancy,' said Peter, 'I must have been suffering from in-growing resentment. It's better to let these impulses have their natural outlet, don't you agree? Repression is always so dangerous. Bunter, find Master Bredon's snake for him and return it carefully to the furnace-room. It answers to the name of Cuthbert.'

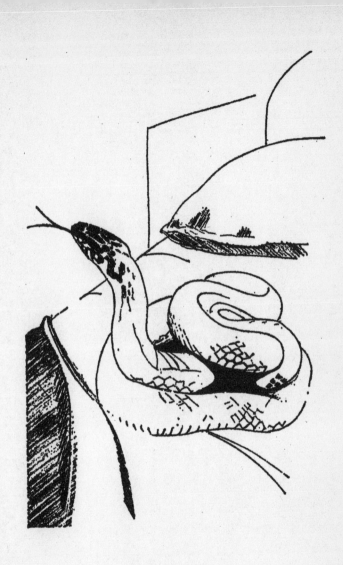

WIMSEY, PETER DEATH BREDON, D.S.O.; *born* 1890, *2nd son of* Mortimer Gerald Bredon Wimsey, 15th Duke of Denver, and of Honoria Lucasta, *daughter of* Francis Delagardie of Bellingham Manor, Hants.

Educated: Eton College and Balliol College, Oxford (1st class honours, Sch. of Mod. Hist 1912); served with H.M. Forces 1914/18 (Major, Rifle Brigade). *Author of:* 'Notes on the Collecting of Incunabula', 'The Murderer's Vade-Mecum', etc. *Recreations:* Criminology; bibliophily; music; cricket.

Clubs: Marlborough; Egotists'. *Residences:* 110A Piccadilly, W.; Bredon Hall, Duke's Denver, Norfolk.

Arms: Sable, 3 mice courant, argent; crest, a domestic cat couched as to spring, proper; motto: As my Whimsy takes me.

A short biography of Lord Peter Wimsey, brought up to date (May 1935) and communicated by his uncle Paul Austin Delagardie.

I AM asked by Miss Sayers to fill up certain lacunae and correct a few trifling errors of fact in her account of my nephew Peter's career. I shall do so with pleasure. To appear publicly in print is every man's ambition, and by acting as a kind of running footman to my nephew's triumph I shall only be showing a modesty suitable to my advanced age.

The Wimsey family is an ancient one – too ancient, if you ask me. The only sensible thing Peter's father ever did was to ally his exhausted stock with the vigorous French-English strain of the Delagardies. Even so, my nephew Gerald (the present Duke of Denver) is nothing but a beef-witted English squire, and my niece Mary was flighty and foolish enough till she married a policeman and settled down. Peter, I am glad to say, takes after his mother and me. True, he is all nerves and nose – but that is better than being all brawn and no brains like his father and brother, or a mere bundle of emotions, like Gerald's boy, Saint-George. He has at least inherited the Delagardie brains, by way of safeguard to the unfortunate Wimsey temperament.

Peter was born in 1890. His mother was being very much worried at the time by her husband's behaviour (Denver was always tiresome, though the big scandal did not break out till the Jubilee year), and her anxieties may have affected the boy. He was a colourless shrimp of a child, very restless and mischievous, and always much too sharp for his age. He had nothing of Gerald's robust physical beauty, but he developed what I can best call a kind of bodily cleverness, more skill than strength. He had a quick eye for a ball and beautiful hands for a horse. He had the devil's own pluck, too: the intelligent sort of pluck that sees the risk before he takes it. He suffered badly from nightmares as a child. To his father's consternation he grew up with a passion for books and music.

His early school-days were not happy. He was a fastidious child, and I suppose it was natural that his school-fellows should call him 'Flimsy' and treat him as a kind of comic turn. And he might, in sheer self-protection, have accepted the position and degenerated into a mere licensed buffoon, if some games-master at Eton had not discovered that he was a brilliant natural cricketer. After that, of course, all his eccentricities were accepted as wit, and Gerald underwent the salutary shock of seeing his despised younger brother become a bigger personality than himself. By the time he reached the Sixth Form, Peter had contrived to become the fashion – athlete, scholar, *arbiter elegantiarum – nec pluribus impar*. Cricket had a great deal to do with it – plenty of Eton men will remember the 'Great Flim' and his performance against Harrow – but I take credit to myself for introducing him to a good tailor, showing him the way about Town, and teaching him to distinguish good wine from bad. Denver bothered little about him – he had too many entanglements of his own and in addition was taken up with Gerald, who by this time was making a prize fool of himself at Oxford. As a matter of fact Peter never got on with his father, he was a ruthless young critic of the paternal misdemeanours, and his sympathy for his mother had a destructive effect upon his sense of humour.

Denver, needless to say, was the last person to tolerate his own failings in his offspring. It cost him a good deal of money to extricate Gerald from the Oxford affair, and he was willing enough to turn his other son over to me. Indeed, at the age of seventeen, Peter came to me of his own accord. He was old for his age and exceedingly reasonable, and I treated him as a man of the world. I established him in trustworthy hands in Paris, instructing him to keep his affairs upon a sound business footing and to see that they terminated with goodwill on both sides and generosity on his. He fully justified my confidence. I believe that no woman has ever found cause to complain of Peter's treatment; and two at least of them have since married royalty (rather obscure royalties, I admit, but royalty of a sort). Here again, I insist upon my due share of the credit; however good the material one has to work upon it is ridiculous to leave any young man's social education to chance.

The Peter of this period was really charming, very frank, modest and well-mannered, with a pretty, lively wit. In 1909 he went up with a scholarship to read History at Balliol, and here, I must confess, he became rather intolerable. The world was at his feet, and he began to give himself airs. He acquired affectations, an exaggerated Oxford manner and a monocle, and aired his opinions a good deal, both in and out of the Union, though I will do him the justice to say that he never attempted to patronise his mother or me. He was in his second year when Denver broke his neck out hunting and Gerald succeeded to the title. Gerald showed more sense of responsibility than I had expected in dealing with the estate; his worst mistake was to marry his cousin Helen, a scrawny, over-bred prude, all county from head to heel. She and Peter loathed each other cordially; but he could always take refuge with his mother at the Dower House.

And then, in his last year at Oxford, Peter fell in love with a child of seventeen and instantly forgot everything he had ever been taught. He treated that girl as if she was made of gossamer, and me as a hardened old monster of depravity who had made him unfit to touch her delicate purity. I won't deny that they made an exquisite pair – all white and gold – a prince and princess of moonlight, people said. Moonshine would have been nearer the mark. What Peter was to do in twenty years' time with a wife who had neither brains nor character nobody but his mother and myself ever troubled to ask, and he, of course, was completely besotted. Happily, Barbara's parents decided that she was too young to marry; so Peter went in for his final Schools in the temper of a Sir Eglamore achieving his first dragon; laid his First-Class Honours at his lady's feet like the dragon's head, and settled down to a period of virtuous probation.

Then came the War. Of course the young idiot was mad to get married before he went. But his own honourable scruples made him mere wax in other people's hand. It was pointed out to him that if he came back mutilated it would be very unfair to the girl. He hadn't thought of that, and rushed off in a frenzy of self-abnegation to release her from the engagement. I had no hand in that; I was glad enough of the result, but I couldn't stomach the means.

He did very well in France; he made a good officer and the men liked him. And then, if you please, he came back on leave with his captaincy in '16, to find the girl married – to a hardbitten rake of a Major Somebody, whom she had nursed in the V.A.D. hospital, and whose motto with women was catch 'em quick and treat 'em rough. It was pretty brutal; for the girl hadn't had the nerve to tell Peter beforehand. They got married in a hurry when they heard he was coming home, and all he got on landing was a letter, announcing the *fait accompli* and reminding him that he had set her free himself.

I will say for Peter that he came straight to me and admitted that he had been a fool. 'All right,' said I, 'you've had your lesson. Don't go and make a fool of yourself in the other direction.' So he went back to his job with (I am sure) the fixed intention of getting killed; but all he got was his majority and his D.S.O. for some recklessly good intelligence work behind the German front. In 1918 he was blown up and buried in a shell-hole near Caudry, and that left him with a bad nervous breakdown, lasting, on and off, for two years. After that, he set himself up in a flat in Piccadilly, with the man Bunter (who had been his sergeant and was, and is, devoted to him), and started out to put himself together again.

I don't mind saying that I was prepared for almost anything. He had lost all his beautiful frankness, he shut everybody out of his confidence, including his mother and me, adopted an impenetrable frivolity of manner and a dilettante pose, and became, in fact, the complete comedian. He was wealthy and could do as he chose, and it gave me a certain amount of sardonic entertainment to watch the efforts of post-war feminine London to capture him. 'It can't,' said one solicitous matron, 'be good for poor Peter to live like a hermit.' 'Madam,' said I, 'if he did, it wouldn't be.' No; from that point of view he gave me no anxiety. But I could not but think it dangerous that a man of his ability should have no job to occupy his mind, and I told him so.

In 1921 came the business of the Attenbury Emeralds. That affair has never been written up, but it made a good deal of noise, even at that noisiest of periods. The trial of the thief was a series of red-hot sensations, and the biggest sensation of the bunch was when Lord Peter Wimsey walked into the witness-box as chief witness for the prosecution.

That was notoriety with a vengeance. Actually, to an experienced intelligence officer, I don't suppose the investigation had offered any great difficulties; but a 'noble sleuth' was something new in thrills. Denver was furious; personally, I didn't mind what Peter did, provided he did something. I thought he seemed happier for the work, and I liked the Scotland Yard man he had picked up during the run of the case. Charles Parker is a quiet, sensible, well-bred fellow, and has been a good friend and brother-in-law to Peter. He has the valuable quality of being fond of people without wanting to turn them inside out.

The only trouble about Peter's new hobby was that it had to be more than a hobby, if it was to be any hobby for a gentleman. You cannot get murderers hanged for your private entertainment. Peter's intellect pulled him one way and his nerves another, till I began to be afraid they would pull him to pieces. At the end of every case we had the old nightmares and shell-shock over again. And then Denver, of all people – Denver, the crashing great booby, in the middle of his fulminations against Peter's degrading and notorious police activities, must needs get himself indicted on a murder charge and stand his trial in the House of Lords, amid a blaze of publicity which made all Peter's efforts in that direction look like damp squibs.

Peter pulled his brother out of that mess, and, to my relief, was human enough to get drunk on the strength of it. He now admits that his 'hobby' is his legitimate work for society, and has developed sufficient interest in public affairs to undertake small diplomatic jobs from time to time under the Foreign Office. Of late he has become a little more ready to show his feelings, and a little less terrified of having any to show.

His latest eccentricity has been to fall in love with that girl whom he cleared of the charge of poisoning her lover. She refused to marry him, as any woman of character would. Gratitude and a humiliating inferiority complex are no foundation for matrimony; the position was false from the start. Peter had the sense, this time, to take my advice. 'My boy,' said I, 'what was wrong for you twenty years back is right now. It's not the innocent young things that need gently handling – it's the ones that have been frightened and hurt. Begin again from the beginning – but I warn you that you will need all the self-discipline you have ever learnt.'

Well, he has tried. I don't think I have ever seen such patience. The girl has brains and character and honesty; but he has got to teach her how to take which is far more difficult than learning to give. I think they will find one another, if they can keep their passions from running ahead of their wills. He does realise, I know, that in this case there can be no consent but free consent.

Peter is forty-five now, it is really time he was settled. As you will see, I have been one of the important formative influences in his career, and, on the whole, I feel he does me credit. He is a Delagardie, with little of the Wimseys about him except (I must be fair) that underlying sense of social responsibility which prevents the English landed gentry from being a total loss, spiritually speaking. Detective or no detective, he is a scholar and a gentleman; it will amuse me to see what sort of shot he makes at being a husband and father. I am getting an old man, and have no son of my own (that I know of); I should be glad to see Peter happy. But as his mother says, 'Peter has always had everything except the things he really wanted,' and I suppose he is luckier than most.

PAUL AUSTIN DELAGARDIE.

DOROTHY L. SAYERS

THE NINE TAILORS

When his sexton finds a corpse in the wrong grave, the rector of Fenchurch St Paul asks Lord Peter Wimsey to find out who the dead man was and how he came to be there.

The lore of bell-ringing and a brilliantly-evoked village in the remote fens of East Anglia are the unforgettable background to a story of an old unsolved crime and its violent unravelling twenty years later.

'She brought to the detective novel originality, intelligence, energy and wit.'   P. D. James

'She combined literary prose with powerful suspense, and it takes a rare talent to achieve that. A truly great storyteller.'   Minette Walters

'In the realm of mystery stories there are four books which everyone should read . . . *The Nine Tailors* is the best.'   Sinclair Lewis

NEW ENGLISH LIBRARY
Hodder & Stoughton

If you have enjoyed this book, you might like to find out about the Dorothy L Sayers Society.

Founded in 1976, with members throughout the world, the Society:

- holds regular meetings throughout the year and a Convention every summer
- produces wide-ranging research and writings on Sayers and her varied literary output
- has published her Poetry, Letters and *The Lord Peter Wimsey Companion* – the ultimate enquire-within about the man and his times.

To find out more and how to join, visit our website: www.sayers.org.uk

Or write to The Dorothy L Sayers Society at:

> The Dorothy L Sayers Centre
> Witham Library
> Newland Street
> Witham
> Essex CM8 2AQ

The Wimsey Arms are reproduced by kind permission of Giles Scott-Giles on behalf of the late C W Scott-Giles.